D.F.

Aberdeenshire
COUNCIL

Aberdeenshire Library and Information Service
www.aberdeenshire.gov.uk/libraries
Renewals Hotline 01224 661511

21

HEADQUARTERS
2 0 SEP 2016   14. MAY 19.
          2 2 JUN 2020
HEADQUARTERS
2 0 OCT 2016
    1 9 JAN 2017

                    1 8 JUN 202.

2 9 DEC 2017

0 9 FEB 2018

1 6 MAR 2018
- 6 DEC 2018

D1429089

The Venom of Valko

For any bounty hunter, the most valuable prize around was the bounty on the Valko Kid. It was a fortune and as such it brought out the lowest of the low to try and claim it.

On one moonlit night Sheriff Colby Masters led his posse to a narrow canyon ridge to wait. It had been rumoured that Valko was headed to the town of War Smoke. The large moon was at its brightest when the posse suddenly saw the rider below them. A horseman clad all in black, atop a magnificent white stallion that thundered through the canyon. It had to be him.

But none of them knew that before the night was over they would all taste *The Venom of Valko*. . . .

By the same author

The Valko Kid
Kid Palomino
The Guns of Trask
The Shadow of Valko
Palomino Rider
The Spurs of Palomino
South of the Badlands
The Masked Man
Palomino Showdown
Return of the Valko Kid
The Trail of Trask
Kid Dynamite
War Smoke
The Sunset Kid

The Venom of Valko

Michael D. George

A Black Horse Western

ROBERT HALE · LONDON

© Michael D. George 2010
First published in Great Britain 2010

ISBN 978-0-7090-9062-5

Robert Hale Limited
Clerkenwell House
Clerkenwell Green
London EC1R 0HT

www.halebooks.com

The right of Michael D. George to be identified as
author of this work has been asserted by him
in accordance with the Copyright, Designs and
Patents Act 1988

ABERDEENSHIRE LIBRARY & INFO SERV	
3033939	
Bertrams	17/12/2010
WES	£13.25

Typeset by
Derek Doyle & Associates, Shaw Heath
Printed and bound in Great Britain by
CPI Antony Rowe, Chippenham and Eastbourne

For my friend movie star Monte Hale, the last of the singing cowboys who sadly has left us. He was a truly nice man and respected by all.
Thanks, Monte.

There will be some mighty fine singing in Cowboy Heaven now the choir is complete. We'll all miss you.

PROLOGUE

There was death brewing along the remote stretch of land which separated the grassy range from the desolate plain. Dust drifted from the jagged peaks which loomed to both sides of the canyon as the dozen horsemen reached its highest point. They reined in to rest their lathered-up mounts on the slender trail which had brought them to this perilous place. A place which only bushwhackers would seek out in order to use their deadly weaponry upon unsuspecting prey far below. This was where slaughter could be dished out without fear of retribution.

Real men faced their foes. These men chose to ambush and massacre theirs. It was always safer that way however good you might be with your rifle or six-shooter.

The fiery heavens above them battled against the inevitable coming of darkness. Only Satan knew what dwelled within their heartless souls as the sky grew redder until it looked as though it was aflame. The dying embers of sundown glanced across their Winchesters as they slowly drew them from their saddle scabbards and checked that their magazines were full and ready.

Stars started to appear across the sky as it darkened. A few at first, then thousands. The sun sank far beyond the place where the posse had decided to make camp and await their chosen victim. There were a hundred better places for long riders to make camp but none which offered the unscrupulous band a better view of what lay below their high vantage point.

For this was the only place between the towns of Waco and War Smoke where the range narrowed and forced all travellers to move through a high-sided canyon. Anyone headed to War Smoke from Waco had three choices: to journey a hundred miles out of their way, climb the walls of the canyon or ride through its unprotected length. The dozen horsemen knew that the odds were in their favour that the man they sought would choose the last of these. He had no reason to suspect that the deadly barrels of those who were intent on his destruction would be waiting for him.

It had been two days since the riders had arrived at Waco aboard the long cattle train from Dodge. They had known that the locomotive had managed to overtake the rider as it negotiated its way back to the more southerly cattle towns. No horse with blood in its veins could keep up the steady pace that a lumber-fuelled iron horse could manage. They arrived in Waco, purchased the best horseflesh available, then headed out on their deadly quest.

All because of a telegraph message their leader had received from a bounty hunter who had information to sell. Information which told them of an overheard conversation between an outlaw and a man he had wrongly trusted.

Two long days of hard riding had brought them to the only place where they were certain they could intercept the wanted outlaw with the handsome reward upon his head.

Dead or alive was always a hard temptation to resist but when added to a reward of $25,000 it became something most men could only ever dream about. A fortune to be had by anyone with the ability to shoot straight.

None of the posse knew the truth of the outlaw they had doggedly sought for nearly a week. None of them would have cared even if he had known that the Valko Kid was an innocent victim of mistaken identity. All that mattered to them was the bounty money. A fortune. And men seldom find the strength to resist a fortune.

They had been told that Valko was heading toward War Smoke for some unknown reason. They knew that the posters said he was nearly thirty, dark-haired and close to six feet in height. He was also known to wear black and ride a white stallion. No one had ever learned what his true name was but they had all heard the name of the Valko Kid. An outlaw worth $25,000 in hard cash.

A rider who always wore black and rode the most powerful white stallion anyone had ever seen would not be easily missed in this landscape, they all thought.

Even perched up high on the side of a canyon wall it would be easy to spot a white horse as it galloped through the narrow gap below them. Even the darkness of night would be no shield to a rider with such a mount.

Not with a big sassy moon above them.

If their information was correct Valko would be forced to use the canyon to reach his goal. The twelve men all looked up at the bright moon above them. Its eerie light illuminated the entire length of the canyon floor like a morning sun. If Valko came this way he was a dead man.

Not even the Valko Kid could ride unseen this night, they all silently told themselves.

Sheriff Colby Masters was, like so many others of his profession, a man who knew that death was only a whisker away if you were honest. A little bit further away if you weren't quite so honest. Masters had never been a truly honest soul and as he grew older he realized that his chances of ever living long enough to retire was becoming as thin as the wisps of hair on his head. Retiring with any money was an even slimmer hope. Then something happened which altered everything in the lawman's mind.

Almost by accident he had learned that the famed Valko Kid was in these parts. Masters knew that this might be his final chance to make it rich. Rich enough to live the way he had seen others live. In luxury.

In this barren land $25,000 did not come along often.

It had to be his.

His alone.

The sheriff glanced briefly over his broad shoulder at the men behind him. A rough, sorrowful bunch. The eleven deputies looked nothing like men who should have ever been allowed to wear the tin stars they had pinned to their top coats. But they had been duly sworn in by the ambitious lawman personally. Masters had hand-picked them all. Not for their honesty, but for more practical reasons. Each of them was a keen shot with both rifle and handgun. None of them had the wits most new-born kittens were born with. Each was as corrupt as the next. Each was perfect for the job they had been employed to do.

Hand-picked.

A perfect bunch of mindless killers who would obey anyone who growled loud enough. Masters sure knew how to growl.

The sheriff dragged his saddle and blanket off the back of his exhausted mount and dropped them on to the ground. He inhaled the stale, dry range air which even the high peaks seemed unable to sweeten.

A wry smile etched across his face.

The Valko Kid was close. He could sense it.

Maybe it was the price on the young outlaw's head that he could taste. Whatever it was he smiled. Wide and long. The others behind him had no idea of the fortune which Valko was worth. They would not see a penny of it, Masters told himself. Not one red cent of that reward would be split with any of them. They were not his partners, they were his cannon fodder. If the outlaw managed to fire back when they started their onslaught Masters knew he had enough deputies to absorb every one of Valko's bullets.

As moon crept ever higher across the black velvet above them, Masters sensed that the valuable outlaw was getting closer. There was no sound to be heard except that of the whistling wind which taunted the ragged spires. The information he had been given about the outlaw was from an impeccable source. Black Jasper Tooley was not just a bounty hunter but a man who had become rich from knowing things others did not know. Masters knew that if he said Valko was headed this way, he was.

Tooley never made mistakes.

The sheriff rubbed his unshaven face and kicked at the dusty edge of the trail. He watched as dust floated down into the deep chasm. The bright moonlight illumined the long trail between the mountainous sides of the canyon. There was nowhere to hide down there. Nowhere at all.

Masters tilted his head and nodded to himself.

'C'mon, Kid!' he whispered. 'Make me a rich old man!'

ONE

There had been no warning of what lay ahead within the confines of the long moonlit canyon as the horseman steered the mighty white stallion into its mouth. He thundered along the dusty trail which was flanked by the high-sided rocks at a pace designed to outrun any followers. But there were no followers. His enemies lay a few miles ahead perched like vultures upon the high trail amid the shadows. Each with his rifle in his hands. Dust rose from the hoofs of the white stallion. It hung in the canyon as the rider urged his trusty mount to find greater and greater speed. This was no place to dawdle. No place to allow one's horse to catch its second wind. The rider knew only too well from past experience that where there were high-sided rock faces, there was always the risk of being ambushed.

The horseman leaned even further over the neck

of the intrepid stallion. He balanced in his stirrups to take the weight off its back and kept urging the animal on. There were few horses anywhere which could have so effortlessly obeyed its master without the use of spurs. Yet this rider never wore spurs. Never thrust their sharp brutal spikes into his mount. There had never been any need. The stallion could run faster than most other horses a quarter of its age. The rider gripped his reins in his hands and rocked in his stirrups over the neck of the charging animal.

Instinct told him that this was probably the most dangerous part of his long journey. Instinct also told him that he had to complete its course as quickly as possible. Only when he reached the grassland beyond would he willingly allow the mount to slow. Only then would the sweat stop flowing from the band of his black Stetson. Only then would his heart cease pounding like a Cheyenne war drum.

The rider glanced up and screwed his eyes against the bright moon almost directly ahead of him. Another two miles or so were left of this dangerous trail, he told himself. Then the tall grass and the trees would give him cover.

Thunderous echoes filled the canyon from the hoofs of the muscular animal beneath him as it ploughed on in response to its master's urging. They grew louder as the canyon grew narrower. Yet the rider heard nothing except his own heartbeat.

15

Another mile had disappeared into the dust behind the long flowing white tail of the powerful stallion. Only eight furlongs remained and then they would escape this treacherous place, the horseman thought. Another few minutes and he could relax. The town of War Smoke was now less than a half day's ride away.

So close and yet still out of reach.

He was going to make it, he told himself. His fears had been wrong. For all its black shadows this eerie moonlit place was just another canyon, he resolved.

Colby Masters swung his rifle around and trained it on the rider who was approaching fast. His posse followed his lead and nursed their weaponry into their shoulders. Each barrel aimed at the speedy black-clad horseman as he got closer.

Maybe if his heart had not been keeping pace with the constant pounding of his horse's hoofs the rider might have heard the rifles being cranked. Maybe if he had looked upward to his right he might have seen them bathed in moonlight. Maybe one of those first shots might not have found its mark.

So many maybes.

It had been like an explosion as the twelve Winchesters opened up at almost the same moment. A cloud of gunsmoke filled the air around the riflemen as the deafening echoes rebounded off the solid canyon walls. Another volley shook the canyon as

16

another dozen bullets rained down from the highest point along the craggy peak.

The rider had felt his arm nearly torn from his body as one of the first bullets cut into him, whilst others smashed into the sand all around him. The stallion stumbled as it felt its master roll sideways from the force of the lead which had hit him. Then the horse responded to the yells of the rider and began to gallop again.

More bullets sliced down through the smoky air like crazed hornets. They ripped into the ground and the opposite rockface. Chunks of stone showered over the white stallion as it raced away.

The horseman clung on for dear life and looked back. He could see them as they frantically fired again. Only the thickening gunsmoke protected him now, he thought. So much smoke from so many rifle barrels hung in the air up between the canyon spires and the floor of the canyon. It hid him from almost certain death.

The rider went to draw one of his guns but his right arm was broken. He glanced at it and saw the blood pumping from the wound. He wrapped the reins around his left hand and hauled it tight before rising again in the stirrups. Pain racked through his every sinew but he knew that he had to try and give the powerful stallion a chance of finding more speed. Somehow he managed to remain astride his horse as it obeyed his yells and found that extra turn of pace.

Dust floated up high as the animal continued on.

More lethal bullets cut down around them. Now the air smelled of gunsmoke. The rider balanced as his arm hung limply at his side and screamed again at the charging white animal below him.

'Run, Snow! Get us out of here!'

Yet there was no reason to yell at the stallion. More than most it knew how to avoid the lead of its master's foes. It had only been its own strength which had kept the law from capturing him for a more than a decade.

Now the horseman was not steering his mount. Now it was the white horse who found its own path. It ignored the swaying bleeding man atop it and began to zigzag as yet more bullets smashed into the ground behind them.

The stallion lowered its head and snorted. Like a raging bull it headed for the swaying grassland which it could now see, as though it were charging a matador's red cape.

Just as they reached the end of the canyon where the boulders grew smooth and smaller another bullet caught the top of the rider's shoulder. It ripped a chunk of flesh from the rider's already busted arm.

Again he rocked in agony. Somehow he managed to stay atop the thundering creature as blood droplets floated in the moonlight. The bullets could no longer reach them but the stallion kept on charging. The range of tall grass and wide-girthed trees greeted them but neither the horse nor its master seemed to notice.

It was as though all they could hear was the sound of bullets echoing all about them.

They ploughed onward.

TWO

A cloak of black clouds covered the night sky above the sprawling town. Neither stars nor the brilliant moon seemed to be able to penetrate it. But it mattered little to those who roamed around within the busy confines of War Smoke. The light of a hundred coal-tar lanterns illuminated its main streets as the six-horse stagecoach wound its way off the range and into Front Street. The sound of a cracking whip from the driver was a familiar sound to those who lived in War Smoke. Those who watched the driver as he slowly began to rein in recognized the familiar bearded face of Luther Figgis and gestured to the old-timer. The long dusty carriage and its equally begrimed horses were expertly guided toward the Overland Stage depot. The springs of the vehicle made it rock as the weather-beaten Figgis hauled back on the hefty array of reins and pushed his right boot against the brake pole. The coach slowed to a gentle halt against the raised platform outside the well-lit office.

The shotgun guard had already clambered on to the roof of the stagecoach and was untying the ropes which secured the passengers' bags even before the vehicle had been brought to a stop.

Depot manager Clevis Booker walked out of his office and checked his pocket watch under the swaying porch lantern. He reached across from the raised platform and opened the coach door before touching his temple to the three weary passengers as they slowly disembarked.

In well-rehearsed fashion he said the same thing to each of the trio of passengers.

'Thank you kindly for travelling with Overland.'

The coach driver pulled out a chunk of tobacco and a penknife as he rested on the high seat with his leg still on the brake pole. He began to slice the end of the chewing tobacco into mouth-sized lumps.

'Reckon there's trouble brewing out there, Clevis boy.'

Booker looked up at the hair-covered face. 'What you talking about, Figgis?'

'Trouble.' Figgis repeated the word before looping the reins around the brake pole and relaxing his leg. 'Out yonder.'

Booker looked up at the bearded driver. 'What

you gabbing about? You look OK. The stage looks OK. What kinda trouble you talking about?'

The driver sighed. 'Out there on the trail between here and Waco. We seen 'em. A mean, ornery-looking bunch with more rifles than Custer. I figure that's trouble.'

'You seen any trouble?' Booker rubbed his jaw.

'Nope. But we sure seen a lot of long riders.' Nate Swayne, the guard, handed the bags down to the depot manager who in turn gave them to the waiting passengers. 'At least a dozen or more heavily armed riders was to the south of the stagecoach trail for over an hour just before sundown.'

'Outlaws?' Booker questioned.

Figgis cut a chunk of tobacco and placed it into his toothless mouth. 'If they was outlaws they sure steered clear of us. Whatever they wanted it weren't our strongbox. They was after something, though. Mark my words. Trouble.'

Swayne had been a guard with the stagecoach company for nearly five years and had seen his share of trouble during that time. He clambered down and stood beside the thin, tall Booker and then rested a gloved hand on the open coach door. His eyes narrowed as he slowly closed the door.

'Whatever they are, they were headed straight up the canyon wall like goats!' Swayne added his contribution. 'Why'd anyone want to ride up the side of the canyon for? It don't lead no place.'

'It sure don't,' Booker mumbled.

'Bushwhackers,' Figgis said as he spat a lump of black goo at the ground. 'No sane varmint would ride up that mountain just to take in the scenery. They gotta be intending on bushwhacking some poor critter.'

Booker checked his watch again. It was still several hours before midnight. 'Maybe I ought to go tell the marshal about them riders you seen. What you reckon?'

Figgis spat again, then ran a stained sleeve across his beard. 'I figure Matt might be interested, Clevis. He likes to be kept in the picture when it comes to things like that.'

Booker nodded.

'That's what I'll do then. I'll go tell him.'

Figgis handed the strongbox to the depot manager, then followed it down to the platform. He watched the liverymen as they walked to the coach and began to unhitch the team from the vehicle.

'What you figure them riders were doing, Nate boy?' Figgis asked his companion.

The shotgun guard shrugged. 'Beats me! Bushwhacking seems a fair bet though.'

Booker had just locked the strongbox up in his office safe and returned to the two coachmen who were standing under the lantern. He still looked troubled even though he had no idea why. He lowered his head until it was between Swayne and Figgis.

'Them riders might give the morning stage trouble, boys,' he observed. 'It goes through the canyon, unlike this 'un.'

Swayne nodded long and slow. 'Yep! They might be getting themselves set upon that canyon wall to wait for the morning stage, Clevis. Yep! I reckon you might be right.'

Booker looked anxious. 'And the morning stage always carries gold coin for the First National Bank.'

Figgis raised a bushy eyebrow. 'That's gotta be it, Clevis. Them varmints are holed up waiting for the morning stage. It wouldn't stand a chance in the canyon if'n it does get bushwhacked.'

Swayne gave a sigh. 'I'm sure glad I ain't riding shotgun on that 'un.'

'Me too.' Figgis chewed. 'A man could get himself killed in the canyon. Ain't no place to hide up on that running board if'n folks start shooting down on you.'

The conversation between the pair of seasoned coachmen only added fuel to the anxious Clevis Booker's already blazing imagination.

'Sweet Lord! That's right! I'll go have me a word with Marshal Fallen right now. We can't let one of our stagecoaches get robbed.' Booker frantically nodded to himself and looked at the marshal's office across the wide street. There was movement behind the lowered blinds. Booker mopped the sweat from his face, jumped down to the street and began to march towards the office. 'This is awful! We could all lose our jobs if somebody got a strongbox.'

'Clevis sure gets fired up.' Swayne remarked as he watched the depot manager hurry towards the marshal's office.

'That boy'll fret himself into an early grave, Nate,' Figgis said drily.

'Yep!' Swayne agreed.

With a twinkle in his eyes, Figgis patted Swayne's arm. 'Beer?'

'Yep!' Swayne grinned.

'Good!' The wily old man with the bandy-legged gait led his younger companion away from the coach. 'You're buying, boy.'

'Figures!' Swayne laughed loudly.

The two coachmen stepped down from the depot platform to the street and headed towards the nearest saloon. Neither they nor Booker had noticed or paid any attention to the youngest of their passengers. A passenger who still hovered less than ten feet from the coach in the shadows at the corner of the boardwalk.

The soberly dressed young man turned his jacket collar up and then pulled down on his hat brim to hide his features from prying eyes. He had listened to their every word.

Silently the young man turned away and carried his small bag in the opposite direction, towards the High Top hotel.

He had more important business.

THREE

The two lawmen looked at one another as the depot manager at last talked his way out of the marshal's office. An almost hysterical volley of words had flowed from Booker's mouth and it had taken nearly thirty minutes to calm him down. The marshal, Matt Fallen, well over six and a half feet tall, rested the palm of his left hand on the door and shook his head. He looked across at his smiling deputy and sighed.

'Clevis sure ain't happy, Elmer,' Fallen said.

'He's as nervous as a steer in a butcher's shop, Marshal Fallen.' Elmer Hook stood and walked to the stove, upon which a coffee pot was resting. 'Ya think them riders Clevis was ranting about are gonna rob the morning stage like he fears?'

'Maybe.' Fallen walked to the window and raised its blind. He stared out at the street. It was bathed in the light of many lanterns. Even darkness could not slow the pace of folks within the boundaries of War Smoke. 'They might be going to bushwhack some poor critter who makes the mistake of riding through the canyon, Elmer. Either way I reckon there'll be blood spilled before we get much older.'

Elmer filled both their mugs and handed one to the marshal. 'I don't reckon on there being a dozen riders like he said. That Luther Figgis can sure bend and stretch the truth a whole lot when he's a mind to stir up someone's mustard. I bet there was only a few riders, coz I sure ain't never heard of that many riders all in one bunch. Have you?'

Fallen blew into the mug and stared through the steam at his deputy. 'Yep!'

Elmer blinked hard. 'You have?'

'Sure enough. A posse can have twice that many.' Fallen suggested. 'They tend to go for quantity rather than quality.'

'What would a posse be doing in these parts?' The deputy swallowed some of his powerful brew. 'We ain't had no telegraph wires about there being any dangerous outlaws on the loose.'

Fallen rubbed his chin. 'Right enough we ain't. You'd think that if anyone had formed a posse they'd have wired me. I am the marshal, after all. Maybe they *are* a gang of desperados just like Clevis said.'

The deputy snapped his fingers. 'I got me a plumb

good idea! Why don't we just tell Clevis to send the morning stage on the longer trail around the canyon instead of through it, Marshal Fallen?'

'We could.' Fallen exhaled thoughtfully. 'That wouldn't make us any wiser, though. Them horsemen would still be out there making all sorts of plans.'

Elmer nodded and took another sip of his beverage. 'Reckon so but I don't figure you'll want to do anything about them though. Ain't against the law for folks to ride up a canyon. They ain't done nothing illegal yet.'

Fallen picked up his gunbelt, strapped it around his hips and then checked his seven-inch-barrelled Colt. 'I don't hanker for someone to get themselves killed before I do something, though. We better go find out who and what they are.'

Elmer knew the tall man well enough to recognize the curiosity in the marshal's tone. 'What if they are outlaws, Marshal Fallen? If we go riding out there to the canyon they might shoot at us! Hell! We might get ourselves killed.'

Fallen swilled the last of his coffee around his mouth and then managed to swallow it. He cleared his throat, grabbed his hat, then looked at the younger man.

'That might be right but I'd be a pretty poor lawman if I didn't go and try to find out what twelve heavily armed riders are doing in my jurisdiction, Elmer. And there's only one way to find out.'

Elmer lowered his mug and placed it on his desk. 'You serious, Marshal Fallen? You going out there?'

Fallen smiled. 'Not alone I ain't.'

The deputy knew what Fallen meant. He moved to the door ahead of his superior and gripped its handle.

'I'll go get our horses from the livery.'

Fallen smiled even wider. 'Good boy, Elmer. You're starting to learn.'

Elmer briefly paused and turned as he stepped out on to the boardwalk.

'My ma ain't gonna like it if we gets ourselves good and killed, Marshal Fallen. Well, if *I* gets myself good and killed, anyways.'

The marshal did not respond. He pulled his jacket free from the wall peg and slowly put it on. Fallen stepped out into the cool air, turned and locked the office door behind him. He then began to follow the younger man who was headed in the direction of the livery stables.

Elmer's muttered complaints hung on the evening air.

The powerful white stallion did not show any hint of its fifteen summers as it thundered across the flat range with its wounded rider slumped over its saddle horn. The animal had never been found wanting when it came to stamina. It knew that the bullets which traced through the darkness were deadly, that it had only one option and that was to leave its pursuers eating the dust from its hoofs.

It had been said that there was no faster horse anywhere in the West than the one belonging to the wanted outlaw known as the Valko Kid. The pure-white muscular thoroughbred stallion called simply Snow had always managed to outrun all who had challenged it.

Until now.

Now they were gaining. It had been an hour since the rider clad in black had felt the bullets tear into his flesh and had slumped over the horn of his saddle. He had dug his boots into the stirrups and with his left hand gripped the reins for all he was worth.

And he was worth $25,000. Hard cash. Dead or alive.

More than a decade earlier, when both the outlaw and his handsome horse had been younger, they had been able to make fools of every posse who had tried vainly to capture that prize. Now age was creeping up on them both. Time had suddenly turned on them and was winning. The cruel passage of time had taken the pace out of the once seemingly matchless horse's legs.

The horseman clung on and felt his blood soaking his shirt until it stuck to his flesh. He turned his head and stared out through the darkness at his pursuers as he felt the stallion racing below him. The moonlight showed the blood stains which now covered the back of the white animal.

The rider saw the clouds ahead of them through dust-filled eyes. He urged the horse on towards the storm. Nothing could be seen below those clouds. There, he told himself, he might just manage to find sanctuary.

The posse had somehow managed to ride down from their high perch on the summit of the canyon and reach the range in record time. The rider wondered how they could have done so. The trail must be a treacherous one even in daylight, let alone in the middle of the night.

The wounded horseman cursed the moon and the men who wanted him dead. He knew that to them he was not a man. To them he was a piece of meat. A lucrative piece of meat.

A trophy.

Again the stallion somehow managed to find renewed strength as it expertly sidestepped the trees, brush and swaying grass and forged onward. Again the bullets erupted from their rifles and sizzled like burning embers around him.

The storm clouds were spreading like spilled black

paint above him. The rider gritted his teeth and hung on with his left hand as his broken right arm moved limply at his side. He inhaled and could smell the scent of rain in the otherwise dry air. It was raining from those black clouds, he told himself. Rain would wash away the tracks left in the wake of the hoofs of his trusty steed.

He had to reach that storm.

Once more the eerie bluish air lit up as red-hot tapers of lethal lead passed within a whisker of the stallion. He held on to the reins even tighter and lowered his hand until it was forcing down upon the saddle horn. He steadied himself and then leaned to his left so that he could look back.

His eyes were tight and he strained to see his followers more clearly. At first he only saw the lead riders. Their tin stars glinted in the bright moonlight. Then he saw the others. They were riding wider of the lead riders. Five, eight, ten, twelve of them.

'Damn it all!' he growled as he returned back to face what lay ahead. 'A dozen of the critters! They must really want that reward money.'

The horseman heard the blasting again. The flashes of lead rocketed to both sides and then he felt the pain again. New pain which was even worse than the original wound. He arched and somehow kept balance. He had been hit again. This time the bullet had caught him in his hip. The rider buckled over the horse and only willpower kept him astride the massive creature as it raced away from the lethal lead which sought to strike at them again.

It had felt like a mule kick.

His legs went weak. The rider could no longer remain standing in his stirrups. Now he was forced to sit on the saddle.

Now he could hear the sound of their horses' hoofs above those of his stallion. Now they were closing in for the kill. The rider steered the horse hard to his left towards a small narrow dry cleft in the rocks. He raised his hand, then swung the ends of the long reins down hard. They made a cracking sound like a whip and the powerful animal fearlessly leapt down into the gulch.

Trees could be seen ahead. Beyond them there were smooth boulders. Then came spires of jagged thin rock which pointed to the sky like fingers. The moonlight cut down the edge of the rocks, making them look as though they had been touched by the brush of some heavenly artist. The rider was exhausted and in agony but he refused to quit. If his horse could battle on then so could he.

As the white blood-splattered stallion reached the smooth boulders the horseman heard the posse as they drove their own mounts down into the gulch behind him.

He knew that the horse beneath him would keep

on galloping at breakneck pace until its pounding heart burst from the effort. It would defy its own pain and charge on. It would ignore its own weariness and obey its wounded master until death intervened.

More shots.

They ricocheted off the rocks. Clouds of dust floated in the moonlight. The white stallion charged on. Its hoofs churned up the ground as it ploughed along the arid ravine and navigated between the boulders. But now the pace of the animal was slowing by the second. Ignoring his pain, the rider vainly tried to take his weight off the shoulders of the horse. Now the animal laboured and snorted as at last its own strength evaporated like that of the blood-soaked man in the saddle.

For the first time since the chase had started the shooting seemed to stop. The horseman used his last ounce of strength and steered the horse through a twisting narrow maze of rocks where the moon could not shed light. Bushes taller than both of them covered the top of the rocky haven and gave the horseman a brief sense of hope.

He reined in and felt the horse beneath him nearly collapse. Then as he rested a shoulder against one of the rocks he heard the posse thundering past their hiding-place.

The sound of their hoofs on the stony ground grew fainter and fainter as Colby Masters and his posse forged on. Now they were chasing shadows. Shadows made by the moon and the rocks and the swaying branches of trees. Shadows which were not of his making any longer. The horseman could no longer feel his fingers on his right hand as he released the reins and inhaled deeply.

Had they gone?

The question burned like a branding-iron into his weary, tortured mind. His fingers touched his arm and then his hip. His eyes stared down until they managed to see the blood on his fingertips. He looked down and saw the blood which covered his right pants leg and the horse.

So much blood, he thought.

And all of it was his.

Should he remain here? Was it safe to stay hidden? What if they turned back and retraced their trail. They would find him and his spent horse easily, he concluded. Even though it seemed cruel he had to ask the proud white stallion to try and get them away from this place. To try and find that storm and the rain which would refresh them both as well as wash away their tracks.

Swirling dust hung on the trail as the horseman teased the reins and made the stallion walk backwards out of the narrow hiding-place. The rider hauled the reins to his left and rode in the opposite direction. Now he would attempt to escape the posse amid the boulders which towered above them. The horse tried to respond to the boots of the injured soul upon the saddle and clambered up the stony rise.

'Go on, Snow.' The words encouraged. 'We only got to reach them peaks and they'll never find us.'

Then suddenly another resounding bullet cut through the air from far below the labouring horse. The horse felt the rider in black quake.

The rider said no more.

The dozen riders cleared the high-walled mouth of the rocky haven and charged through the choking dust. The sound of their hoofs echoed all around the area. It sounded like an army more than just a posse, but the horseman did not turn to look.

He heard nothing.

The valiant stallion stopped. Its noble head turned and looked down at the crumpled heap lying in the moonlight a few paces behind its muscular legs. The blood covered half his trail gear.

He did not move.

The posse opened up again. Red-hot rods of deadly lead came spewing out of the dust as the riders closed in on their fallen prey.

But Snow did not flinch. The defiant white steed stood its ground and towered over the fallen man at its feet. It would protect the blood-soaked rider who had brought it to this god-forsaken place. It moved forward, then dragged a hoof across the stony ground as the riders came up the rise through the swirling dust. The closer they got the more enraged the animal got. It gave out a blood-curdling sound, then rose up on to its back legs and pawed at the air.

The stallion wanted them to be afraid. Wanted them to know that it knew that it was their bullets which had brought its rider down.

But the horsemen were not smart enough to be afraid.

They were drunk on the sight before them.

The posse's excited voices filled the air. They were now roaring like ravenous animals. They could taste the hideous flavour that killing brought to some men. The sight of their prey riddled with their bullets excited them.

'He ain't riding so pretty now, Sheriff!' one of the posse chuckled.

'He sure ain't!' another agreed.

'We got him! We got the bastard!' Colby Masters yelled out at the top of his lungs as he dragged rein and stopped his own mount twenty feet from where the stallion stood protecting its bloody master. 'The Valko Kid sure done met his match when he run up against us boys!'

All the riders stopped their horses next to the jubilant sheriff and began to laugh as only men who have just tasted the spoils of their crude handiwork can laugh. Mentally calculating how much bounty the lifeless Valko was worth, Masters hastily dismounted and walked towards the unmoving man in black.

Then the stallion snorted viciously and stopped Masters in his tracks. The lawman looked at the powerful animal and felt his throat tighten. The horse had seemed far smaller at a distance, he silently thought.

Snow rose up again and then brought his hoofs down hard. His eyes widened and blazed in the light of the moon at the sheriff.

'What ya gonna do, Sheriff?' one of the men, named Cy Kent, asked. 'That nag sure looks riled up.'

'He'll stove ya head in, Colby,' Josh Cooper added. 'Watch out! He's mighty angry and no mistake.'

Undaunted, Masters returned to his own mount and pulled his Winchester from beneath the saddle. He cranked its mechanism, then raised the rifle to his shoulder and looked along the length of its barrel until the head of the stallion was in his sights.

'I'm gonna kill that damn horse just like we killed Valko.'

FOUR

The sound of the six-shooter being fired brought every one of the posse to a frozen halt. None more so than Colby Masters who had tasted the dust kicked up by the bullet which had landed at his feet. The bright moonlight lit up the awesome figure who loomed above the twelve bloodthirsty souls, gripping his smoking Colt in his solid right hand. With the storm behind his broad shoulders Marshal Matt Fallen stood firmly on the crest of the rocky outcrop like an eagle surveying his next meal. Sheriff Masters rubbed the dust from his face and glared angrily up at the imposing Fallen.

Then the rest of the posse focused on the marshal's thumb as it clawed back again on his gun hammer until it locked into position.

There was no mistaking that sound. It rivalled the echo of the earlier shot in their heartless souls. For most it meant a warning, for others it always meant death. Fallen remained silent as moonlight danced along the smoking seven-inch barrel. The dozen men did not need to hear him speak, they knew what he wanted.

Fallen had achieved his goal.

Masters' eyes stared at the man who looked like a statue as lightning lit up the heavens behind his mighty frame. For a moment he forgot all about the white stallion who stood between him and the body.

'What the hell are ya trying to do, stranger?' Masters snarled as his posse looked to him for leadership.

Fallen said nothing.

'Who is he, Sheriff?' Cooper whispered across the distance between them.

The sheriff felt his hands begin to sweat up as they clung to the long Winchester. Every sinew in Masters' body told him to swing round and start blasting the rifle's deadly lead up at the large man. But Fallen had a rare look about him. A look which seemed to tell folks that it would be they who would die in a showdown.

'Who are ya?' Masters shouted up at the tall Fallen. 'Who are ya? Speak up or I'll surely kill ya.'

Fallen had his six-shooter aimed straight at the nervous sheriff with the rifle clutched in his hands. For a moment he did not reply, then he began to walk slowly down between the gigantic boulders. Each step was calculated and true. Men like Fallen never took a misplaced step when their lives depended upon it. Even though he could see that all of the men wore tin stars, he still did not trust any of them. He knew that they might swing and begin firing their weaponry at any given moment.

'I asked ya who ya are,' Masters snarled again. 'This is law business and we don't hanker for anyone to interfere. Savvy?'

'The name's Matt Fallen,' the tall man replied in a low drawl. 'United States marshal. What you doing shooting folks in these parts?'

A bead of sweat ran down the face of the sheriff as he forced a smile and lowered the Winchester. He waved a free hand at the others behind him.

'I'm Sheriff Colby Masters and this is my posse.'

Fallen continued to descend the dusty slope. 'I heard of you, Masters.'

Masters smiled. 'Yeah? What you heard about me?'

'I heard you're a no-good skunk,' Fallen replied honestly.

The smile disappeared from the sheriff's face. 'What?'

Fallen reached level ground and paused. His eyes flashed from the horsemen to the sheriff and then to the body before they returned to Masters. He kept the Colt aimed straight at the midriff of the man who held on to the rifle.

'You heard me. What you doing chasing down a man and shooting him in my jurisdiction, Masters?' Fallen narrowed his stare. He did not blink. 'I should have been telegraphed about this. I don't like folks riding wild and killing other folks in my territory. Not even if they are sporting tin stars.'

'Nobody talks to me like that.' Masters spewed out his words.

'Wrong!' Fallen corrected. 'I just did. I ought to force that rifle down your throat as well.'

Masters pointed with his rifle at the blood-soaked body beside the still snorting horse. 'Hold on a darn minute. That's the Valko Kid lying there. I got news that he was headed through here and I had me no time to tell anyone about me forming a posse.'

Fallen raised an eyebrow. He still did not blink. 'The Valko Kid in these parts? I thought he rode further south-west than this.'

Masters was about to approach the marshal, then he thought better of it. He remained glued to the spot as slowly all of his riders dismounted.

'That might be so but I was told that Valko was headed through Waco on his way to War Smoke.' Again the sheriff pointed with his rifle at the body. 'There's the proof of the pudding, Fallen. Valko! Dead! We just killed a wanted outlaw who's bin terrorizing folks for years. Ain't no call for ya to get ornery with us.'

'Maybe.'

'Ya blind? He's there.' Masters shouted.

Fallen edged sideways towards the body. The white horse reared up again and lashed out with its deadly hoofs. The marshal stopped and briefly looked at the posse.

'Somebody rope that critter,' he demanded.

'I was gonna kill the damn thing when you turned up,' Masters said wryly. 'I'm still willing to waste a bullet on the blasted thing. That horse is as loco as its master was.'

Fallen's look burned the smile from Masters' face. 'I don't cotton to folks killing horses. Horses are mighty valuable around these parts.'

The sheriff looked at his followers. 'Any of you good enough with a cutting rope to get the better of this nag?'

There was a silence. None of them seemed either willing or able to do what Masters requested. These were not men who could do anything except back-shoot, drink and brag. Little else.

Then a voice cut through the air behind the posse. It startled them. Every one of the posse swung around and saw the deputy standing above them with his primed scattergun in his hands.

'I'll do it, Marshal Fallen,' Elmer said loudly.

They stared at where Elmer was standing with the

big twin-barrelled weapon aimed at them. Like the marshal, the youngster looked more than willing to use his scattergun.

'Who in tarnation is that?' Josh Cooper asked.

'My deputy. Mr Elmer Hook,' Fallen answered.

Masters looked back at Fallen. 'I thought you seemed mighty brave for a man with only one gun. Twelve targets and only six bullets. Should have known you had an ace up your sleeve.'

Fallen nodded to Elmer. The deputy began to move down the dusty rise towards the angry horse as the marshal returned his cold stare to the figure of the sheriff.

'I'd not have bin troubled by any of them riders of yours, Masters. If the shooting had started I'd have just killed you and they'd have high-tailed it.'

'You reckon?' the sheriff asked.

Fallen nodded. 'Yep!'

'What makes you so certain?'

'Looks like that poor critter on the ground took all your lead in his back,' Fallen remarked, without a hint of fear. 'I'd say that you and this bunch of yella misfits like to back-shoot. Ain't one of you that could face a man in a showdown.'

There was a fury in the face of the sheriff. 'I've killed men for saying less than that, Fallen. Hear me?'

'You back-shoot them, Masters?' Fallen asked. 'Bet

you never seen the whites of their eyes.'

After handing his scattergun to Fallen, Elmer removed a rope from one of the posse members' saddles, then fearlessly approached the fiery animal, which was still standing guard over the twisted figure on the ground. The deputy made a loop and then began to twirl the rope over his head as he closed in on the stallion.

'He sure is a big old fella and no mistake,' Elmer observed as he kept swinging the rope above his head.

'Careful, Elmer,' Fallen said from the corner of his mouth.

'He'll get his head stoved in.' Cy Kent laughed.

'Won't that be a pretty sight?' Masters said with a grin.

Fallen inhaled deeply. 'There ain't a better man with a rope than Elmer here, Masters. Reckon you ought to tell them boys of yours to keep their mouths shut before I get a tad angry.'

Elmer threw the lasso. It floated through the moonlight until it neatly encircled the neck of the white stallion. The deputy pulled back and tightened the loop until it was firmly secured around the horse's throat. He then began to walk backwards away from the tormented animal. When he reached a sturdy smooth boulder Elmer looped the rope end around it and began to take in the slack.

'What's he doing?' one of the watching posse asked.

'What am I doing? I'm getting me some leverage here so he don't pull my arms out of my sleeves,' Elmer grunted as he displayed his expertise at handling creatures far bigger than he would ever be.

Every eye watched the young deputy as he slowly subdued the powerful stallion into submission. Every eye except those of Fallen. They remained firmly glued to Masters.

Using skills he had learned during his days of trail-driving Elmer slowly reduced the length of the rope around the horse's neck by making the stallion charge him. He would wait until there was slack in the rope and then loop it over the immovable boulder. Time and time again the deputy courageously repeated the action until there was a mere ten feet of rope remaining between the horse's head and the boulder. The fiery stallion could no longer rear up and lash out with its lethal hoofs. Now it was trapped beside the rock, unable to get close to the blood-soaked man who still lay motionless on the sand.

'I figure he's under control now, Marshal Fallen,' Elmer announced as he staggered back to the side of his boss.

'Good work, Elmer,' Fallen said.

'What ya intending to do, Marshal?' Masters defiantly asked as Fallen approached the man in black. 'Ya gonna steal the bounty on Valko's head? That ya game? Is it?'

Silently Fallen tossed the scattergun into Elmer's hands and then knelt down. The moonlight made the bloody trail gear of the crumpled body shine. Fallen reached out and gripped the man's shoulders. He eased the body over until it was face up.

Fallen inhaled deeply. He then tilted his head and glanced at his deputy. 'Keep that gun aimed at them, Elmer. They make a move for their weapons and you blast them with both barrels. Understand?'

'I understands just fine, Marshal Fallen,' Elmer answered.

Masters was furious. He wanted to approach the marshal but knew that the deputy would obey his deadly instructions if he even tried. 'What ya playing at, Fallen? We killed the Valko Kid and he was an outlaw. Ya treating us like we are the outlaws with bounty on our heads. Valko was wanted dead or alive.'

Fallen pulled the black Stetson off the head of the man who lay at his knees. His eyes stared at the face long and hard.

'Valko's wanted dead or alive, but not this poor varmint.'

The words chilled Masters and his followers. The sheriff made as though to move forward, then he looked at Elmer with the cocked double-barrelled weapon in his hands. 'Let me go to Fallen.'

Elmer smiled. 'Toss ya guns aside and you can go any damn place ya want, Sheriff. Careful though. This old scattergun got hair triggers.'

Colby Masters eased his guns from their holsters and dropped them at his feet. 'OK?'

'OK.' The deputy nodded whilst keeping the hefty gun pointed at the rest of the posse.

Masters marched across the sand and looked down at the face before rubbing his neck nervously.

'I don't get it,' he admitted. 'We chased Valko. That's the Kid's white horse right there. Who the hell is this?'

'There are a lot of white horses in this territory, Masters.' Fallen said drily. 'Don't mean that every rider on top of the things are the Valko Kid.'

The sheriff stared at the face of the man lying beside Fallen's knees. This was the face of a man about fifty. The moonlight highlighted the greying hair at his temples.

'Who is he?'

'Whoever he is he ain't a thirty-year-old.' Fallen eased the damp vest away from the bloody shirt and located a hidden pocket. He found a wallet and eased it free. 'Maybe this'll tell us who you and your back-shooters gunned down.'

'But he was running away,' Masters muttered.

'Why would he run away?'

'Reckon I would spur mighty hard if I had me a small army shooting at me.' Fallen opened the wallet. He saw a card with gore covering its edge. The marshal withdrew it and turned it so the moonlight allowed him to read.

'What's it say?' Masters grunted. 'What's it say, Fallen? Does it name him? Who is he?'

Fallen looked up at the frustrated sheriff. 'Yep. It names him OK. This is retired US Marshal Clem Everett. You and your boys gunned down a lawman.'

Masters staggered backwards a few steps.

He was shaking. Not through regret or guilt but a toxic mixture of fear and anger. He knew that he and his band of men could be arrested for murder. An honest jury might find them guilty and that meant their necks would be stretched.

'We didn't know, Fallen,' Masters said.

'Reckon I believe you.' Fallen said regretfully as he rested a hand on Everett's chest. 'You boys were after the Valko Kid and drooling over the price on his head. Why would you kill an old retired lawman? There ain't no profit in that kinda mistake.'

Masters felt a sense of relief wash over him. He cleared his throat and ventured closer to the kneeling marshal again. 'Ya mean that ya ain't gonna arrest us for murder?'

Fallen shook his head. 'Nope.'

Elmer turned and looked at Fallen. 'But these dirty back-shooters gunned down an innocent man, Marshal Fallen. That's murder in my book.'

'It might be if Everett was dead.' The marshal looked at both men in turn. 'Somehow this old lawman is still alive.'

'What?' Masters stared down at the man lying in a pool of his own blood. There was no sign of movement. 'Are ya sure about that, Fallen?'

'Yep.' Fallen nodded and looked up at the face of the sheriff who loomed over him. 'Must be your lucky day.'

Masters wanted to run. His men wanted to run even more.

'Now if I was you I'd gather them men together and ride. Ride fast because Marshal Everett might not make it and if he dies I'd have to change my mind.' Fallen said.

Masters did not require telling twice. He rushed to his men and plucked up his guns from the sand. They all grabbed their reins and steadied their mounts.

'Mount up! We're riding!' he shouted.

Within a mere heartbeat the twelve men had thrown themselves on to their saddles and turned their horses away from the gruesome scene.

Elmer walked to where Fallen knelt and leaned over as the horsemen galloped away from their brutal handiwork.

'He sure looks dead and no mistake, Marshal Fallen. Yep! I seen a lotta dead 'uns who looked more alive that he does.'

'You ain't too far from being right, Elmer.' Fallen slid his arms under the blood-soaked frame and then slowly rose back to his feet. He had Everett cradled in his mighty arms as if the retired lawman weighed no more than a child. 'Reckon you can untie that stallion without getting trodden to death? I think we have to get him on that brute if we want to get him back to War Smoke.'

Elmer gulped and looked anxiously at the stallion. 'He looks a little calmer now. I oughta be able to keep him sweet long enough for you to get that poor critter back on his saddle. If I'm lucky that is.'

Fallen whistled. Their own horses came over the rise and cantered down towards them.

As Elmer cautiously approached the large horse he noticed the look on the marshal's face. 'What ya thinking about, Marshal Fallen?'

'I heard a tale a while back that Clem Everett resigned for some reason a year or so ago and hooked up with Valko.'

'Why would he do that?'

'And why would he be dressed up to look exactly like Valko?' Fallen added. 'Even riding a white stallion just like the Kid is reputed to do.'

'That's just asking to be gunned down by bounty hunters and the like.' Elmer said. 'He must be plumb suicidal.'

'Clem Everett is a lot of things but he ain't suicidal, Elmer,' Fallen corrected. 'Hurry up and get that horse free. We have to get this old fool to Doc Weaver if he's to stand a chance of living until sunup.'

As Elmer loosened the rope from around the boulder his expression altered. 'If Everett is here where in tarnation do ya figure the real Valko Kid is, Marshal Fallen?'

Fallen was thoughtful. He eased Everett on to the saddle of the white stallion, then stepped into the stirrup and mounted the horse behind the unconscious man. He gathered up the reins and allowed the horse to turn.

'You get our horses and ride as fast as you can back to town. Tell Doc to get some water boiling, Elmer,' Fallen instructed as he urged the stallion on, carefully holding Everett between his strong arms.

Elmer leapt on to his horse and grabbed the reins to the marshal's mount. He spurred and thundered away as Fallen guided the stallion after him.

With each stride of the long legs of the white horse the marshal pondered the question posed by his deputy.

Where was the Valko Kid?

FIVE

There were only five of them now. Sheriff Colby Masters had seen most of his deputized henchmen flee as soon as they had ridden away from the place where the dying Everett lay. Maybe it had been the fear of a hangman's noose around their necks that had made them drive their spurs deep into the flanks of their mounts, or it could have been the knowledge that it was doubtful they would ever get a share of the bounty on the head of the very valuable Valko Kid. As Masters defiantly steered his horse into the outlying streets of War Smoke he knew the truth. They had been afraid of Fallen.

Men like Matt Fallen were rare. They could scare most men by simply raising an eyebrow. The men who had deserted Masters knew that the marshal was willing and able to do a lot more than just raise an eyebrow.

Rain had started to fall over the normally dry ground. The sheriff pulled back on his leathers, stopped his horse at the far end of Front Street and rubbed his unshaven jowls. He glanced back and wondered how long it would take Fallen and his cohort to return to town. With the almost lifeless body in tow it ought to take a while, he thought.

Long enough to take a look around town?

Long enough to see if Valko was here?

Masters nodded in answer to his own silent questions.

Cy Kent, Josh Cooper, Trey Withers and Bo Davis surrounded their leader and waited as they always waited. These were men with little or no brains. They did what they were told to do as so many men tend to do. They never questioned. They simply obeyed like well-trained animals.

The sheriff looked at them in turn. 'Reckon we're a tad shy on numbers now that Fallen bastard done scared off the others but there's enough of us to do what we gotta do.'

Cooper screwed up his face and gave the storm clouds over their shoulders a fearful look. 'Whatever we gotta do can we do it someplace where them lightning rods can't git us, Sheriff?'

'That storm is coming this way and no mistake,' Bo Davis added. 'We ought to git these nags under cover.'

Masters sniffed the air and then looked to his right at a winding street which curled like a drunken rattler. He raised a hand and pointed a finger.

'I figure the livery stables are thataway.'

The others nodded in agreement.

The five riders turned their horses and tapped their spurs into the flesh of their already exhausted mounts. They rode across the wide Front Street and into the twisting narrow confines of the alley. Their noses told them this was the way to the livery stables.

The rain came down harder.

The storm drew closer.

Like a battle between ancient Nordic gods the sky over War Smoke erupted into life. Black brooding clouds were lit up as the lightning pulsed its brilliant flashes whilst keeping pace with the unseen heavenly drummers who deafened the mere mortals who listened and watched far below. When the full fury of nature vented its wrath on mere mortals or their creations it was usually beyond imagining. No human could have devised a weapon as deadly as that which brewed in the soup of a good storm. Nothing was sacred to the lightning forks.

When storms came to the vast expanses known collectively as the West, they were big. Big and often deadly. Little had a chance of survival if struck by the white-hot rods of lightning. Rolling balls of tumbleweed would erupt into flame as the splintered arcs of death sought and found the earth. If a man were struck by a shaft of white death only ashes tended to remain.

Even the bravest of men shied away from venturing out when the gods were doing battle.

The violent storm had drifted across the town of War Smoke just before midnight. The driving rain pounded down constantly and made every brick and wooden plank shine as though coated by varnish. Few would have chosen to be out on the range away from the relative safety of War Smoke's many porch overhangs and shingle roofs, but for a handful there had been little or no choice. Men had to travel to or from places and if they got caught in the middle of the storm they were at its mercy.

The storm had been brewing for days amid the intensifying heat and every man, woman and child knew that there was only one sure way for the air to sweeten. They were helpless, as they had always been helpless.

Doc Weaver stood sucking on his pipe beneath his porch overhang outside his office, watching the sky. He had seen more storms than he could recall during his long life and this one seemed no better or worse than all those which had gone before it. He struck a match, shielded its flame and lit the plug of tobacco in his pipe bowl. Smoke drifted from his mouth and added more stain to his moustache.

Front Street was almost empty. Men had found their chosen place this night and would remain there until the angry tempest eventually passed over War Smoke.

Only a couple of horses stood tethered to hitching rails along the wide thoroughfare. They spooked and dragged at their reins, vainly battling to free themselves, but the old doctor knew that even drunken cowboys always tied their reins securely. For most men their horse was their most valuable asset.

The lightning flashed again.

The entire length of Front Street suddenly looked as though it was bathed in sunlight. Then the flickering light vanished as swiftly as it had arrived. Doc waited and puffed and then felt the boardwalk beneath his weathered shoes rock as the thunder exploded.

His wrinkled old eyes were about to glance back up into the heavens when they caught a glimpse of a familiar rider heading straight towards him. Weaver pulled the stem of the pipe from his mouth and spat at the wet street as his stare narrowed.

It was a soaked to the bone Elmer Hook, who was standing in his stirrups and forcing his horse on through the driving downpour. Doc rubbed his chin thoughtfully and wondered why the young deputy was trailing Matt Fallen's mount beside him.

The deputy hauled back on his reins and leapt down. He secured both horses' reins to the hitching pole and stepped up under the porch. Then Elmer shook himself like an old hound dog that had been caught out in a shower. Steam drifted off the two horses and filled both men's nostrils.

The smell was mighty sound.

'What you doing with Matt's horse, Elmer?' Doc asked as he looked at the bedraggled creature beside him. 'He ain't hurt someplace, is he?'

'Marshal Fallen's bringing in a lawman who got himself shot by a posse, Doc,' Elmer explained as his hands searched for a dry scrap of clothing he could wipe his face with. 'The man's nearly dead and I don't reckon he'll be alive by the time the marshal gets him here.'

'Shot?' Doc tapped the pipe bowl against the nearest wooden upright and watched as the smouldering tobacco danced in the rain before reaching the ground.

Elmer nodded. 'Two or three times by the looks of it.'

'I'll get a large kettle of water on my stove.' Doc pushed the hot pipe into his coat pocket and turned. His hand opened the office door and he entered with the deputy on his heels. 'Shot by a posse? This is one unlucky lawman by the sounds of it, boy.'

'Unlucky ain't a big enough word for that poor

59

critter.' Elmer sniffed at the air. Then his eyes saw the coffee pot on top of the black stove. The deputy rushed and plucked it away as the elderly physician pumped water into a large kettle. Elmer filled a tin cup and then allowed the heat to warm his hands as he inhaled the fumes of the beverage. 'Ya know the funny thing?'

Doc laboured to the stove and placed the kettle on its flat top. 'Don't seem to me there ain't nothing funny about this whole sorry tale, Elmer.'

Elmer sipped at the coffee. His eyes brightened. 'He was dressed like the Valko Kid.'

Doc paused for a moment. 'Who?'

'Valko,' the deputy continued. 'He's a real bad 'un. I seen his circulars in the marshal's office. Killed a whole heap of folks and is worth a fortune in bounty.'

'I never heard of him.' Doc opened the metal door of the stove and peered inside. He then picked up a log from a basket and pushed it into the flames. 'Seems a tad odd for a lawman to go around dressed like a bandit. No wonder he got himself shot.'

'Seemed a little odd to me as well, Doc.' Elmer finished the coffee and refilled his cup. 'Marshal Fallen said that he's heard that this Marshal Clem Everett had hooked up with Valko a ways back and they was riding together.'

Doc Weaver closed the stove door and straightened up. His wrinkled eyes stared at the deputy.

'What was the name of that lawman, Elmer?'

'Clem Everett.' The deputy nodded. 'Real old-lookin'. About your age, I'd wager.'

'Clem!' Doc looked as though he had just been kicked in the groin as he ambled to the younger man and paused. His face was ashen. 'Clem Everett?'

'That's right.' Elmer looked at the doctor and lowered the cup from his lips. 'You know him?'

Doc nodded silently. 'Yep. I sure do know old Clem Everett, Elmer boy. Mighty fine lawman as I recall.'

'Funny you heard of some tuckered-out old marshal and you ain't heard of the Valko Kid, Doc,' Elmer observed. 'Valko's done famous.'

'I've heard about him, boy,' Doc admitted heavily. 'Nothing good and that don't fill me with anything but loathing. When you spend half your life digging lead out of folks it's hard to see any good in folks that kill for no reason. By all accounts this Valko Kid is just another one of them Billy the Kid types. A crazed killer.'

Elmer leaned over the far shorter man. 'Then how come Clem Everett rides with him?'

Doc's eyes darted to the young man's face. 'Clem would never do such a thing. Ride with vermin? Never. Never!'

'Easy, Doc,' Elmer pleaded. 'You'll bust a gut.'

61

'Clem is as honest as Matt,' Doc insisted.

'Ya gotta be wrong, Doc.'

The old face reddened. 'How would you know?'

'Marshal Fallen told me so.' Elmer gave a nod that was intended to end the disagreement but failed to curtail the old rooster beside him.

'I don't care what Matt told you, Elmer,' Doc fumed. 'I happen to know old Clem. He'd never ride with a wanted outlaw.'

'Ya know him that well?' Elmer picked up the coffee pot and filled his mug again.

'A long while back before I ever came to this neck of the woods me and Clem were good friends,' Doc recalled. 'We even went fishing together.'

Elmer blew into the steam of his beverage. 'Marshal Fallen don't usually get things wrong, Doc.'

Doc slammed his hand down on the table he was preparing for his next patient and glared at the deputy. 'Matt got it wrong this time. Right?'

Elmer silently nodded.

Suddenly the sound of hoofs out in the street grew louder than that of the pounding rain which beat down on War Smoke porch overhangs. Weaver's eyes flashed to the open doorway as he lit more lamps and placed them around the table.

'Sounds like Matt's here,' Doc said. 'Go take a looksee.'

Elmer walked to the door and saw Fallen

approaching on the white stallion. He was still holding the unconscious Everett before him as he guided the mount towards Doc's office.

'They're here OK. I'll go help Marshal Fallen, Doc.'

'Yeah. You do that, boy.' Doc sighed heavily before whispering to himself, 'And let's hope Clem is still alive for me to try and help.'

From down the street the five remaining members of the posse paused outside War Smoke's best drinking hole. They watched the white stallion pass them on its journey to the small office where the lean deputy waited.

'It's that big marshal, Sheriff,' Withers noted, touching the shoulder of the sheriff.

'We might still be in luck.' Cooper said.

'Yep. Looks like that critter we plugged might still be alive.' Masters spat at the ground and then led his men into the Red Dog saloon. 'C'mon, boys. We'll, start in here.'

The four deputies did not object. The swing doors rocked on their hinges.

SIX

It was a short walk from the High Top hotel to the busy Golden Garter saloon. The legs of the young man in the neat suit covered the distance in short time. The saloons were noisy but nowhere as deafening as the claps of thunder which kept on shaking the buildings of War Smoke. Yet it was not the taste for either beer or whiskey which had brought the stranger to this town, it was something far more personal.

Something for which he was willing to risk his life.

He rested a hand on the swing door of the saloon and glanced over its brightly painted surface into the crowd. The tobacco smoke indicated a place where all the comforts that lonely men seek could easily be found.

But this lonely man sought something far more important.

His blue eyes stared at the gamblers and the towns-folk before drifting to the scantily clad females who hovered around the saloon's interior like vultures surveying fresh carcasses.

The one he desperately sought would never be found in this sort of place, he thought.

But where was she?

Where was Mary White?

Three months earlier he had ridden back to Indian Ridge just to find her to discover whether the rumours about her ill health were true. To find out whether other rumours were also true. But she had gone and taken her child with her, according to old Walt Carey the sheriff of that small remote town. It had been eight years since he had last held Mary White in his arms and lied to her.

He had to lie and she had understood.

When you are a hunted man you draw flies. Gun-toting flies. There was no way he would have risked her to satisfy his own happiness. It had taken every scrap of willpower for him to ride Snow away from her that day. A day which was carved into his memory with pain and regret. Had he not been a man branded with the crimes of another he would have stayed.

He could have stayed.

Eight long years and he had still not managed to clear his name. He was still wanted dead or alive.

Then by chance a few months back he and his trail pal Clem Everett had run into an old friend, the burly blacksmith called Lars Olsen in Laredo. Lars had told him the grave news concerning Mary's illness and the even more disconcerting news about the child.

The brief union he had shared with Mary had been fruitful.

Guilt had haunted Valko ever since. He knew how hard it must be for an unmarried woman to raise a child anywhere. The Kid wondered if she had suffered at the tongues of those who are always quick to point down from their self-made pulpits at people whom they secretly envy. Then there was the small boy who had probably been branded for the passionate indiscretions of his parents.

Valko had to find her and his son. He looked around the street for a hint. This was where he had been told he would find her.

But where were they? He prayed he was in time.

It had not been easy getting to War Smoke. Valko had heard that the law was vigilant in these parts in and around War Smoke, and that it had one of the best marshal's to be found anywhere. That was when he and Everett had hatched their plan to try and buy the Kid some time. Time to locate Mary and his son before he himself was discovered. It had been Everett who had come up with the idea of their exchanging roles. Everett knew that the white stallion would lead the guns away from the outlaw and purchase Valko that precious time.

If Walt Carey and Lars Olsen were right time was at a premium. Even a day might make the difference between life and death.

Mary's death.

The Kid felt a shiver trace his spine. It had nothing to do with the storm that raged all around him. In Indian Ridge she had been a baker and café owner, he recalled. Would she still be? How ill was she? Maybe she was too ill to bake bread all night and serve vittles throughout the day. His eyes searched for a sign. A baker or a café sign would do. Anything that might lead him to her and the son he had never met and had only just learned about.

Then, as a gust of wind blew the cold rain against the side of his face, he turned and looked down the long wide street.

He might have been dressed to resemble a drummer on the lookout for fresh buyers of his wares, but beneath the innocent clothing the heart of the Valko Kid beat like a war drum. The young man screwed his eyes against the driving rain as he stepped to the edge of the boardwalk and swallowed hard at the sight which greeted him.

'Snow.' Valko muttered when he saw the white stallion being reined in outside the office of Doc Weaver.

His teeth gritted when he realized that his pal Everett had not steered the trusty horse to the hitching pole. It had been the large man who sat on the cantle behind him.

Lightning flashed.

Everett's face was blank like that of a dead man. Valko rubbed the rain from his features and continued to stare at the unexpected sight. A gut-churning thought hit the Kid low down. Had helping him cost his pal the ultimate price?

Without even knowing he was doing it, Valko began to pace along the boardwalk ever closer to the building opposite where the lamps burned high and bright. His eyes never strayed from the sight which chilled him.

Then he stopped.

He saw Fallen loop his leg over the horse and drop carefully to the ground without ever taking a hand from the retired marshal who was obviously either dead or damn close to it. Then he saw the deputy help the taller man ease their burden off the saddle, then carry Everett into the doctor's office.

Valko's clenched fist rested on the nearest wooden upright and beat at it with troubled abandon.

A thousand fears filled his thoughts.

The largest and most troubling was the one which screamed a question into his mind over and over again. Was Clem dead? Was Clem dead?

The Kid lowered his hand and he stepped back until his spine touched the wall behind him. He inhaled deep and hard. Over and over again, like a panting hound after a real hard racoon-hunt.

Yet Valko knew that he was never the hunter.

Valko had long ago resigned himself to the fact that he would probably always be the hunted. Only death would end that.

But Clem didn't have any bounty on his head, Valko thought.

Clem was an honest soul.

Who could have shot him?

Who could have killed him?

Valko cursed that he had agreed to Clem's plan. The bounty was too high to take risks like that. There was always some dumb bastard who would shoot at a man on a white horse on the off chance that it might be the Valko Kid.

Again the Kid gritted his teeth. He wanted to walk across the street and enter that office and find out for himself whether his friend was dead or alive but every sinew in him told him that was loco. So far he had managed to remain unnoticed but if he entered that door where two men who wore tin stars had carried Clem he would be sticking his neck into a hangman's noose.

He inhaled again, looked up at the boards above his head and tried to settle his instincts down. He

THE VENOM OF VALKO

had to remain calm otherwise everything he and Everett had planned would vanish before he had time to do what he had to do.

The Valko Kid pulled his collar up against the driving rain which was sweeping along Front Street and started back towards the High Top.

Whatever Everett's fate might be, the young outlaw knew that there was nothing he could do to alter its course.

Then he saw a flickering light coming from behind a half-lowered window blind across the wide street near a corner. Valko rubbed the rain from his eyes and adjusted the unfamiliar hat. As a trail of water ran from the brim he saw the faded sign painted on the flaking wall.

'Baker,' he said aloud.

His heart began to race.

The Kid continued to walk. This time faster as he closed down the distance between himself and the building opposite him. A rumbling across the sky went unheard by him. Valko stepped down into the street and headed towards the glowing light which sneaked out from beneath the blind.

Then his nostrils flared.

The aroma of fresh-baked bread filled his soul.

Was Mary in there?

The width of the street seemed to mock his efforts to cross it as he found himself running. The rain beat down like a waterfall cascading from a high cliff edge. It bounced up to chest height but Valko did not notice. He kept on moving and leapt up on to the boardwalk opposite. Another twenty yards, he told himself.

His chest heaved as he came to a halt beside the window.

Its light came out at waist height. He pressed his hand on the wall and slowly knelt down. When his head was level with the bottom of the blind, Valko screwed up his eyes and stared in through the steamed-up glass.

Suddenly a very different noise broke through the sound of the storm. It was a gunshot.

SEVEN

Smouldering debris of wood and brick from the side of the bakery showered over the kneeling Valko Kid. The outlaw turned. His hands went instinctively for his guns but they were not there. Then the youngster remembered that the pair of matched .45s, along with his hand-tooled gunbelt and trail gear, were in his canvas bag in the hotel room he had rented hours earlier.

'Damn it all!' Valko cursed as he ducked another high-velocity rifle bullet. 'Who the hell is that?'

The startled Kid moved to the side when another shot cut through the driving rain. This time it was close. Real close. Shards of brick burst off the wall and hit him square in his face. Valko twisted away and fell across the boardwalk in agony. He rolled off into the street and landed in a large pool of water. He lay there for what felt like an eternity until his face cooled down. Only then did he raise his head and vainly stare away into the distance.

Whoever it was firing the rifle sure had good eyesight, Valko thought.

The street where he lay was becoming like a river as rain kept on pouring down from the black clouds. Then another bullet sought him out. The edge of the wooden walkway shattered as the lump of lead narrowly missed the Kid's left leg.

Rising from what he feared might become a watery grave, Valko rubbed his face and desperately stared down the long wide street to where he just caught sight of another circle of smoke around a rifle barrel. The bullet whizzed over his head, taking the hat as it went. Then another, less than a heartbeat later, tore at the side of his jacket almost ripping it from his body.

'I need my guns,' the Kid snarled. 'This disguise ain't worth a red cent.'

The Kid could not see who was shooting. The rain was like a curtain between them. Then he heard a noise. It was the sound of a man shouting out into the storm. Whatever the voice was saying got lost in the far louder sound of the incessant storm but it seemed to work.

The rifleman suddenly disappeared into a side street, giving the Kid a brief opportunity to rise and run. Valko did both things at breakneck pace.

After reaching the other side of Front Street Valko kept on running for all he was worth along the boardwalks. He did not slow his pace until he reached the High Top hotel and burst into its lobby.

Two men sitting behind newspapers raised their eyes and looked at the bedraggled creature who was panting as he closed the door behind him.

The clerk gave Valko a long stare, then plucked the room key from the rack behind him and held it out as Valko walked across the lobby towards him. Each step left a pool of water in its wake.

'You look kinda damp there, Mr Edwards,' Frank Hale observed with a barely disguised hint of amusement in his tone.

Valko accepted the key and ran his fingers through his wet hair. He forced a smile and nodded.

'It's worse if you lie down in the street,' the Kid said as he turned and aimed his boots toward the stairs that led to all the rooms.

'I heard shooting, Mr Edwards,' Hale said.

Valko paused as his left boot found the first step. His head tilted and his eyes looked at the clerk.

'I heard shooting as well.'

'Was anyone shooting at you?' Hale rested both his hands on the top of the desk in front of him. Both seated men continued to look over their newspapers at the young man who could not have been any wetter.

74

'Why'd you ask?' The Kid toyed with the key in his hand.

'Because you're bleeding, Mr Edwards.' Hale raised a thin finger and pointed to the Kid's right side. 'Quite badly if I'm any judge.'

'I think you're wrong, sir,' Valko retorted.

Hale aimed the finger even further across his desk and pointed sternly at the outlaw's side. 'Look at yourself, young man. You're wounded.'

Valko looked down at his side and to his utter shock saw the crimson stain against his once white shirt. Blood could be seen running down the water-sodden clothing. His fingers touched the hole in his shirt. He recoiled in pain.

'Damn it all if I ain't bin shot,' the Kid muttered in genuine disbelief. 'I never noticed.'

'It is rather cold tonight. I imagine it could numb a reasonable amount of pain.' The clerk nodded and gave a long sigh. 'I would get that looked at if I was you. Doc Weaver's place is on Front Street.'

'Yeah, I seen it,' the Kid said as he thought about his pal already in the doctor's office.

'If you go now and get stitched up you won't be leaving blood everywhere up in your room,' Hale suggested. 'We dislike too much gore in the High Top, Mr Edwards. You understand?'

The Kid looked down at the wound again. It was bleeding badly. He nodded at the clerk and to himself. He turned away from the staircase and tossed the key back into the hands of the clerk. He walked back to the door and turned its brass handle.

Valko said nothing as he went back out into the storm.

The two men with the newspapers in their hands looked to Hale. Hale placed the key back on its hook, shrugged, folded his arms and sat down.

'I'm sure I'd know if I was shot,' Hale said aloud. 'Wouldn't you?'

Both men nodded as their eyes returned to their papers.

With his Colt Peacemaker gripped firmly in his hand, Matt Fallen stood on the boardwalk and squinted out into the driving rain which still lashed Front Street. Elmer stood at his side with his scatter-gun at hip level.

'Who'd ya reckon that was blasting away with that carbine, Marshal Fallen?' the deputy asked as his own eyes surveyed the long street for a hint of where the rifleman had gone.

'I ain't sure, Elmer,' Fallen replied. He edged towards the nearest upright and gazed through the rain down in the direction of the Red Dog saloon where several curious men were watching from the doorway. 'I reckon whoever it was ran up into the alley next to the gaming house when I started shouting.'

'Ya powerful scared me when ya yelled out like that, Marshal Fallen.'

'Whoever it was he's gone now.'

The sky lit up for a few seconds. The lightning seemed to be moving away. Then a slow rumble growled over their heads. The deputy walked to the side of the marshal and rested in the lawman's long shadow.

'Who'd ya figure he was shooting at?' Elmer looked down the long street but the driving rain made it impossible to see anything beyond the Golden Garter gaming house. 'If'n there was someone down there he might have gotten himself real bad shot up.'

Fallen nodded in agreement. 'Yeah. There's only one way to find out if some poor varmint got himself shot, and that's to take a look, Elmer.'

Elmer's face screwed up. 'You ain't gonna make me walk all the way down there, are ya? I'm only just drying out from the ride back into town, Marshal Fallen. A man could catch his death of cold getting rained on all the time.'

Fallen holstered his gun. 'Don't go fretting. I'll go take a look to see what damage was done, Elmer.'

A broad smile covered the deputy's face. It did not last long as the marshal added a footnote.

'You can take our horses to the livery, Elmer.'

'Thanks a whole heap.' Elmer stepped down into

the cold rain and untied both their horses' reins from the hitching pole. He then looked at the large white horse. 'Ya want me to take this big old stallion to the livery as well, Marshal?'

Fallen was thoughtful as he kept looking to where the rifleman had been shooting. He did not look at the deputy as he answered.

'Yep. Get that horse rubbed down and bedded for the night just like ours.' The marshal sighed and placed a hand on the grip of his gun as he started to walk away in the direction of the distant café. 'Best look after that nag in case we have to auction him off.'

'But don't he belong to Marshal Everett?' Elmer held the reins to all three horses in his hands. 'We can't go auctioning his horse off just like that.'

Fallen glanced briefly over his shoulder as his long legs strode away.

'I reckon that horse more than likely belongs to a certain Valko Kid, Elmer.'

Elmer's face looked even more concerned. 'That's worse! We don't wanna go selling his horse in case he turns up looking for it. He might get a tad ornery.'

Standing in the doorway of the Red Dog Sheriff Masters sipped at his glass of rye and nodded to himself. There was a satisfaction in the corrupt man at the sight of both marshal and deputy separating.

'Who'd ya figure that was shooting the street up,

Sheriff?' Josh Cooper asked over the lawman's shoulder.

'I ain't sure,' Masters answered. He turned and walked back into the saloon. 'Whoever it was it's given them two starpackers something else to think about.'

'So they don't give us no heed?' Withers added.

Masters placed his glass down. 'C'mon. Let's head on to that gambling hall down yonder. Valko might be there.'

The five men left the saloon and headed toward The Dice.

EIGHT

Lightning flashed and then spidered down from the clouds and struck at the top of the church tower. The marshal hesitated for a few moments as he watched the wooden cross explode into a million fragments. The stiff breeze took what was left of the burning remnants and scattered them over the town. A swarm of fireflies could not have equalled the sight. Fallen inhaled and then crouched down. He ran his gloved left hand down the wall outside the bakery and felt the impressions where the bullets had torn the brick away. The tall man bit his lower lip and began to study the street scene around him. The rain was slowing but it still masked most of what he knew was there.

This was the place where whatever the rifleman was shooting at had been standing. Questions gnawed at Fallen's craw. Who had been the target and, more important, who had done the shooting?

The lawman straightened up. His eyes narrowed as he turned to face the wind and cutting rain which was still plaguing Front Street.

Who was the target? Fallen asked himself again.

The marshal stepped down off the boardwalk into the deep water and walked out into the middle of the street. He paused and looked up at the sky. The storm had swung full circle and returned to punish the large settlement. He glanced back at the church tower. The fire caused by the lightning strike had been extinguished by the continuous rainfall. Fallen turned his collar up and was about to walk back towards Doc Weaver's office when suddenly a movement to his left attracted his attention.

A figure had crossed in front of the well-illuminated store fronts and was headed into Front Street from the direction of the High Top hotel. It was the first sign of life Fallen had noticed since leaving Elmer ten minutes earlier.

Faster than the blink of an eye the marshal reached for his gun. His fingers curled around its holstered grip as his eyes tried to identify the man whom he saw only in silhouette. Again the sky lit up as another flash of lightning flickered over War Smoke.

In less than the beat of a heart Fallen saw the man as the brilliant light temporarily illumined the figure.

He instantly knew that he was a stranger in a settlement full to overflowing with strangers.

'Hold on there,' the marshal demanded as he slid his gun from its holster and cocked its hammer.

The sodden Valko stopped in his tracks when he saw the star pinned to the top coat of the huge figure with the Peacemaker in his hand. The Kid raised his hands and remained still.

'Anything you say, Marshal.'

'You got good eyesight,' Fallen observed.

'Tin stars ain't hard to see.' Valko sighed.

Even through the driving downpour both men searched one another for answers. There was no way that the marshal could have known that the unarmed figure was in fact the Valko Kid, but years of experience told him that there was something different about this man.

'I don't recall seeing you before, stranger,' Fallen said.

'I came in on the stage.'

'Where you headed?' the lawman asked.

'I'm looking for the doctor of this fair town, Marshal.'

Matt Fallen waded through the water which refused to drain away from the hard-packed earth of the street. He stepped up on to the boardwalk and then looked the sodden figure up and down before releasing the gun hammer and sliding the Colt back into its holster.

'Why you looking for Doc?'

'Somebody took a few potshots at me and I just realized one of them shots got lucky.' Valko lowered his arms and pulled the side of his jacket away from his bloodstained shirt.

'Is it bad?' Fallen enquired with a tilt of his head.

'That's why I'm going to see the Doc.' The Kid smiled. 'I'd hate to be dying and not know about it.'

'You any inkling who was doing all that shooting?' The marshal never took his eyes away from the face of the wanted outlaw.

Valko looked back without blinking. 'Nope!'

'I got me a feeling that I ought to know you, stranger.' The lawman was curious. 'Who are you?'

The Kid shrugged. 'I'm just a drummer trying to rustle up some trade for my bosses.'

'What's your name?' Fallen pressed.

'Roy Edwards.' Valko replied.

The marshal rubbed his lips with the fingers of his gloved left hand. He smiled. 'If you was wearing guns in a fancy shooting rig I'd reckon you fitted the description of someone else, Mr Edwards.'

'Can you show me where I might get myself stitched up, Marshal?' Valko changed the subject skillfully. 'I'm losing a lot of blood here.'

Fallen nodded. 'C'mon. I'll take you there.'

'Much obliged.' The Kid began to follow the tall

lawman along the street beneath the porch over-hangs. Just as they were about to cross the street Fallen paused and looked back at the younger man.

'It'll be interesting to see what you look like when you're all cleaned up, Mr Edwards.'

Valko trailed the marshal across the street towards Doc Weaver's brightly lit office. He did not say a word.

NINE

Cursing every step of the way the bedraggled Elmer
Hook had struggled to lead the mounts through the
back lanes to where the newly constructed livery
stable stood. Each of the horses had fought him over
every inch in their different ways, and he knew it.
Their instincts had told them to run as far away from
the devilish storm as possible. The deputy felt as
though he had been wrestling them rather than just
trying to take them to the relative safety of the livery
stable. His arms hurt and so did every other muscle
in his lean frame. The flashing of deadly lightning
mixed with the deafening thunderclaps had spooked
all three of the horses. When sudden noise exploded
above the heads of any creature it created fear.
Exhausted horses tended to sense danger even more
keenly than most others. That made even the tamest
of them dangerous.

Damn dangerous.

'For pity's sake! C'mon!' Elmer gasped as eventually he reached the wide-open doorway of the tall building where stableman Stanley Bodine watched and waited away from the ceaseless rain.

Elmer hauled the stubborn animals the last few yards and tossed their reins at the burly Bodine.

'Marshal Fallen wants them rubbed down and fed, Stanley.'

Bodine unfolded his muscular arms and picked up the reins from the ground. He could not hide his amusement at the sight of the deputy who had obviously fallen down as many times as it was probably possible to fall down on the short trek from Front Street to his stables.

'Ya kinda muddy there, Elmer,' Bodine remarked as he led the horses into the heart of his building. He tied the reins of all three wide-eyed mounts to the uprights of three empty stalls.

Elmer looked hard at the big man. 'Now don't ya go making fun of me there, Stanley,' the deputy warned the man, who looked as though he could snap tree-trunks with his bare hands. 'I'm in no mood to be mocked. I just wanna git home and put on some dry clothes.'

'Matt should never have gotten you to bring these nags here, Elmer,' the stableman said.

'I'll agree with ya there.' Elmer sniffed and tried to

shake the rain from his soaked frame. 'Them critters done battled with me all the way. Ya'd think I was taking them to a glue factory or something.'

'Ya just plumb feeble, Elmer.' The stableman laughed. 'Ain't a muscle in ya whole miserable body.'

'I got them horses here.' Elmer waved a finger, then he spotted the well-fed forge and its glowing hot coals. He walked to it and felt the heat on his wet clothing. Then he noticed the stalls on the other side of the livery, where five mounts were stabled. He recognized one of them. The one that Sheriff Masters had thrown himself on to before high-tailing it away from Fallen and the bullet-ridden Everett.

'Hey, Stanley. Who was riding that paint yonder?'

'Said his name was Sheriff Masters.' Bodine replied. 'He come in here with four deputies. Worthless-looking bunch with killing in their innards.'

Elmer nodded. 'I didn't think they'd come here after the way Marshal Fallen spooked 'em.'

Bodine looked at the white stallion and could not conceal the fact that he was impressed. He stroked the neck of the tall horse and nodded to himself.

'Where'd ya find this beauty, Elmer?'

The deputy screwed up his eyes and looked at the stallion before turning his attention to Bodine. 'I didn't find him no place, Stanley. A lawman was riding him and got himself all shot up by a posse.

87

The same posse that Sheriff Masters was leading.'

Bodine unhitched the stallion's cinch strap and hauled the saddle free. He walked to the stall behind the animal and hoisted the saddle over the top of the dividing rails between the stalls.

'How'd a lawman get a nag as fine as this 'un, Elmer?'

Elmer walked to the stableman's side, tilted his head and looked at the stallion. 'He ain't that special, Stanley. Just a big old white horse.'

'Ya wrong. He's better than any horse in this stable, Elmer.' Bodine argued. 'I reckon he must be worth a lot. A pretty valuable nag to be owned by a lawman.'

'Yeah?' Elmer scratched his head. 'Ya sure?'

'Look at him.' Bodine kept on nodding. 'This is a pure-bred stallion. Probably from south-of-the-border stock. Spanish or something kin to it.'

The deputy wandered back to the glowing forge and warmed his hands for a few moments. 'Now I know ya joshing. I seen me a lot more better-looking horses than that 'un.'

Bodine turned away from the white stallion and moved to the saddle, which he had balanced on the stall rail. His large hands began to inspect it. 'I reckon this saddle must have cost a pretty penny as well, Elmer. No lawman could have ever afforded this, let alone that nag.'

Elmer sat down cautiously on the edge of the forge and enjoyed the sensation of the heat from the glowing coals warming his rear. He kept watching the stableman.

'What ya looking for, Stanley?'

Bodine did not answer immediately. Then, as his fingers turned the saddle latigo over, he grinned and looked back at the deputy triumphantly.

'What ya smiling about, Stanley?' Elmer asked.

'Who'd ya say owned this horse?'

'I didn't say.' Elmer croaked. 'I just said a lawman had bin riding the thing when he got himself plugged. Why?'

Bodine raised the latigo. 'Look at this.'

Reluctantly Elmer left the warmth of the forge again and walked to the big man, who was holding the latigo in his hands under the light of a lantern. The thin deputy stooped and squinted.

'See it?' Bodine asked.

'Yep.' Elmer felt his jaw drop.

The stableman slapped his thigh. 'I knew this horse and rig had to belong to somebody special. I just knew it! Didn't I say so?'

'Glory be!' Elmer gulped and rubbed his face. 'And there ain't many dudes more special than him.'

Stanley Bodine read aloud the name branded into the leather.

'Valko.'

'That's what it says sure enough.' Elmer nodded and looked Bodine in the eyes. 'Valko!'

Before the burly stableman could utter another word the deputy had turned on his heels and run back out into the raging storm, shouting at the top of his lungs.

'Marshal Fallen! Marshal Fallen!'

Leaving the saddle on its high perch, Bodine wandered to the open doorway and scratched his unshaven chin thoughtfully.

'That boy is sure excitable,' he muttered.

There were no shadows dark enough to hide the soul of the ruthless bounty hunter who had entered War Smoke by the back trail unnoticed earlier that day. Black Jasper Tooley had earned his reputation by killing more wanted men than almost anyone else in the West. It was not his skin that was black but his heart. He killed and he killed good. Some said that it should have been his image on the wanted posters and not those whom he sought and destroyed. For when he killed he used the law to his advantage. If he had ever strayed across that fine line between upholding and breaking the law, there were no living witnesses to betray him.

Tooley had made sure of that.

He had sold the information about Valko being in these parts to Sheriff Masters and then decided to collect the reward money himself. It had been easy to ride wide of Waco on his journey to War Smoke for a man like Tooley. Along the way he had picked up the bounty for a couple of hapless outlaws and pocketed the reward money.

The well-set man who always wore a rough jacket made from the skin of a brown bear he had once shot ambled through the dark alleyways behind the buildings which fronted the town's main thorough-fare. Unseen because he wished it that way, Tooley walked with his Winchester over his shoulder and his hand resting on the grip of his favoured Remington.

Smoke still trailed from the barrel of the rifle as the bounty hunter reached the corner of the Golden Garter's back yard. He checked the gate and smirked. The padlock was rusted and he knew that if he wanted to break it free it would take all of ten seconds.

Little stopped the ruthless Tooley.

He gave out a long sigh and then reached the place where he had left his horse. Soaked to the bone the animal showed all the signs of its brutal master's use of his spurs. The animal was still raw from the gruelling ride to this place. Blood still ran down its belly from the scars Tooley had inflicted.

The bounty hunter slid his rifle into its scabbard, then tore the reins free of the fence post. He led the soaked animal out from the shadows and started to make his way even further along the twisting alley.

The rain continued to beat down on the walking man, who resembled a bear, and his forlorn horse. Yet Black Jasper Tooley did not care about storms or whether he was wet or dry.

All he cared about was the bounty he knew awaited him when he had managed to kill the famed Valko Kid. No disguise could fool the eagle-eyed Tooley. He knew his prey.

He had seen the Kid disembark from the stage-coach earlier and was the only one who had recognized him. But there had been too many people on the boardwalks then. He had waited for his chance and if the rain had not spoiled his aim he would have already been dragging the carcass to the marshal's office to claim the bounty.

Three years had passed since Tooley had last set eyes upon the Valko Kid. It had been a brief, fleeting moment, which he had been unable to capitalize upon at the time. But the face was branded into his memory.

Tooley did not have to see the black trail-gear or the pair of matched .45s or even the white stallion to recognize his chosen prey. He had the Kid's face in his mind.

It was the same with all those he hunted. The image would remain there until his target was dead. Only death erased the images of the men he hunted.

The bounty hunter always seemed to be able to sense when a man was wanted. It was if they had a scent about them. The scent of impending death. As though the grim reaper had branded them with the pungent aroma of doom.

The reward was $25,000, dead or alive.

That one bounty would be almost as much as he had earned in the previous four years of hunting and killing other outlaws. It was more than most men could earn in a dozen lifetimes and it was waiting to be had.

The Kid was in town. Tooley had already unleashed rifle lead at the outlaw and would have finished the job if the marshal had not interrupted.

Tooley knew that Matt Fallen was not a man to allow bounty hunters free rein in his town.

Black Jasper Tooley silently cursed Fallen as he plodded on through the rain. That was one lawman he hated with all his spirit because Fallen could not be bought. Fallen obeyed the law to the letter and that had cost the bounty hunter dearly in the past. Tooley liked lawmen to be afraid of him and never to question the way he went about his gruesome trade, but Fallen was afraid of no one.

Tooley cleared his throat and spat. He then grunted like the creature he had become and kept on walking to where he intended to set his next trap.

Valko had to be killed clean, Tooley told himself.

Otherwise Fallen might interfere and start fanning his hammer at him before he realized what was happening. Some lawmen liked bounty hunters and took their cut of the rewards but the marshal of War Smoke was not that kind.

Fallen was cursed.

Cursed with honesty.

Angrily, Tooley dragged at his reins and snarled again as he waded through the knee-high mud and cut down into an alley he knew would lead him unseen to the far side of the sprawling town.

'C'mon, hoss.'

The far side of War Smoke was a place where rich folks lived and where he knew he could find the one man who could get Fallen out of his hair long enough for him to execute the outlaw he sought.

The horse fearfully followed its brutal master.

TEN

It had taken every scrap of his medical expertise but somehow Doc Weaver had managed to remove all of the bullets from Clem Everett's body and the retired lawman was still alive. The elderly doctor washed his hands in the bowl beside the long table and inspected his work with tired eyes. The water in the white enamel bowl was pink with the blood from the three bullets.

Fallen had been sitting on a hardback chair next to the silent Valko throughout the closing moments of the operation. They had been there long enough to see the last bullet taken from Everett's back and to hear it dropped into the bowl.

'I must be getting better at this damn job, Matt. Clem's still alive.' Doc sighed wearily.

The marshal rose to his full height and rested a hand on the shoulders of the tired doctor.

95

'What's his chances, Doc?'

'Bad, Matt.' Doc sighed heavily. 'My old pal's in a pretty sad way.'

Fallen glanced at Valko. 'Come here, Mr Edwards.'

The Kid stood and walked to both men.

'Show Doc that wound of yours, Mr Edwards.' Fallen said.

Valko did as instructed.

Doc nodded, then looked at the Kid's face. 'I'll put a few stitches in that for you.'

'No cutting?' Fallen asked.

'The bullet went clean through, Matt,' Doc said, 'Tore the flesh up a tad though.'

Valko stared down at his friend lying on the table as the old medical man worked on the gash in his side. He did not show any hint of pain as the needle was pushed into his skin which was then sewn together.

'Will he live?' the Kid asked.

'Hope so,' Doc replied. 'He ain't as young as he used to be though.'

Valko nodded. 'I hope he makes it.'

Fallen studied the outlaw hard with knowing eyes. 'You trouble me, Mr Edwards.'

'Why?'

'Damned if I know why,' Fallen admitted. 'There's something about you that don't quite figure, though. Maybe it's the way you walk. You walk like a man who ought to have a gunbelt strapped around his middle. Your fingers look as though they're ready to curl around a gun grip and haul leather at any moment.'

Valko just looked at Fallen.

'Ya tired, Matt,' Doc scolded.

'Maybe so,' the marshal acknowledged.

Suddenly Elmer ran into the office and grabbed Fallen's arm. Fallen's head turned and he stared into the face of the gasping deputy.

'What's got you all fired up, Elmer?'

The panting Elmer kept pointing in the direction from where he had just run. Eventually he managed to find enough air to speak to the marshal.

'Th . . . that white horse.' Elmer gasped. 'He's belonging to the Valko Kid. Stanley found Valko's name branded on the saddle's latigo.'

Fallen peeled his excited deputy's hands off his jacket sleeve. 'Hell! We already figured that. Old Clem was pretending to be the Kid to steer folks off in the wrong direction.'

'Ain't ya even a little bit surprised?' Elmer's eyebrows rose until he looked like a confused racoon.

'Nope,' Fallen admitted. 'I am a bit curious as to why a seasoned lawman like Everett would help an outlaw, though.'

Doc finished sewing up the side of his unconscious patient and looked at both lawmen. 'I'm wondering where that outlaw is right now, Matt. If Clem was pretending to be Valko then who is Valko pretending to be? And where is he?'

Fallen nodded. 'That thought struck me as well, Doc.'

Elmer sat down and exhaled loudly. 'Ain't nobody surprised that I done found out that white horse is the one that belongs to the Valko Kid? The actual real one. Up until now we was just reckoning that it might be. I found out it's the genuine animal.'

'Good work, Elmer,' Fallen said. He walked out on to the boardwalk and studied the street hard and long.

The Valko Kid followed him on to the boardwalk and was about to continue on his way when he heard the marshal clear his throat loudly.

'You want something, Marshal Fallen?' the Kid asked, trying to remain calm. It was not easy when you were being towered over by a man like Fallen.

'You interest me, Mr Edwards,' Fallen said in a low drawl.

The Kid hesitated. 'Is that so, Marshal?'

Their eyes met.

'That's so, Mr Edwards.'

'Why?'

Fallen straightened up and rested a hand on the porch upright. A smile crossed the face of the seasoned lawman. It was a smile that chilled the Kid.

'You looked concerned when you saw Everett in

there as Doc was digging out them bullets, friend,'
Fallen remarked. 'I got me the impression that you
actually knew that old man. You looked as though
you felt every cut of Doc's scalpel.'

'Yeah?' Valko knew that Fallen deserved his rep-
utaion. He was far more alert than most men who
wore tin stars.

'Yep. And another thing that's bin troubling me is
that you don't look like no drummer I've ever met.
And I've met a whole lot of them.' Fallen watched for
any hint of reaction in the face of the outlaw.

Valko shrugged. 'You've got a suspicious nature.'

Fallen nodded. 'Damn right, Mr Edwards!'

The Kid touched his temple, then turned and
started walking away once more. He knew that Fallen
was watching his every step. He could feel the eyes of
the tall lawman burning into his spine.

Without daring to look back, Valko kept on
walking.

The Dice was the biggest gambling hall in War
Smoke. It prided itself on also being the wealthiest
business in the town. Those who owned The Dice
were rich men but they had long realized that if War
Smoke were not so well policed they could become
even wealthier. The one thorn in the side of all the
businesses along Front Street was Matt Fallen.

The two men who owned The Dice were quite different by nature but exactly the same in their shared greed. Whilst Boston Bill Starkey was flamboyant and always to be found at the gaming tables his partner Rufe Forsyth tended to remain in their offices mulling over their various other business interests.

Colby Masters had started to feel the effects of the second bottle of whiskey he and his four deputies had downed as they sat in a corner away from the busy gambling tables that filled the main room of The Dice.

He lit a cigar and tossed the match at a spittoon. 'I just had me a thought, boys. If we do meet up with Valko how are we gonna know its him?'

'We ain't ever gonna find that Valko Kid critter in this town, Sheriff,' Cooper declared. 'We might as well ride home.'

Before Masters had time to react his bloodshot eyes spotted a well-dressed man heading towards them with a fresh bottle of liquor in his hand. Boston Bill wore the best tailored suits money could buy and this, combined with silk shirts, made him the envy of all those whose ambitions mirrored his own.

The sheriff leaned back in his chair and studied Starkey as the man reached their table. The gambler's smile was wide and a gold tooth could be seen.

'Howdy, gents,' Starkey said as he pulled a chair out and sat down amid the five weatherbeaten men.

'I thought you'd like to join me in a few glasses of imported whiskey.'

Masters pulled himself up on his chair and studied Starkey hard and long. 'Who are ya?'

'I'm Boston Bill, the co-owner of this fair establishment.'

'Why'd ya wanna drink with us, Boston Bill?' Withers asked.

'Yeah,' Masters chimed in. 'We're a tad ripe for sensitive noses like the one I bet you got.'

Boston Bill pulled the cork from the bottle and filled all their glasses before looking into the eyes of the sheriff. 'I seen those stars you boys are packing.'

Bo Davis lifted his glass and sipped at the powerful liquor thankfully. 'We is deputies for Sheriff Masters here.'

'A posse?' Starkey asked.

They all nodded.

'Who are you boys hunting?' Starkey wondered aloud.

'The Valko Kid,' Masters told him firmly.

Starkey shrugged. 'I've never heard of him.'

'He's a real bad 'un,' Cooper added.

The gambler kept refilling their glasses. 'No luck?'

Masters sighed. 'Nope. Ain't had a sniff of the varmint.'

'We did shoot a *hombre* who we thought was him though,' Davis said with a laugh.

101

Starkey looked amused. They all began to laugh.

'Do you think that you might want to earn a few dollars by helping me?' Starkey watched Masters carefully like a man who was trying to tell whether his opponent had a full house or simply a pair of deuces.

'What's a few bucks by your reckoning, Boston Bill?' Masters downed his drink and held the empty glass out to be topped up once more. 'And more important, what ya want us to do to earn them few dollars?'

Starkey grinned wide enough for his gold tooth to catch the lamplight. He stared straight at the man with the sheriff's star pinned to his coat.

'One thousand dollars.'

'I'm startin' to like this town, Sheriff.' Cooper chuckled out loud.

Withers used his fingers and then looked at the others. 'I figure that's two hundred dollars each.'

Masters' eyes lit up. 'To do what, Boston Bill? What do you want me and my boys to do?'

Boston Bill Starkey looked all around him and when he was convinced they could not be overheard he leaned forward across the table and whispered:

'I want you to kill a varmint.'

'A troublesome varmint?' Masters asked with a smile.

'Real troublesome!' Starkey nodded.

'Who?' Masters asked.

The man dressed from head to toe in his finery knew that he might have just found the five pitiful creatures capable of achieving something that he and his partner had longed for.

'Marshal Matt Fallen.'

Withers filled his own glass with whiskey. 'We met that big hunk of sidewinder poison, Boston Bill.'

'I'd sure cotton to bringing him down a peg or two,' Davis said. 'Treated us like we was vermin.'

Starkey leaned back in his chair. He looked straight at Masters. 'Well?'

Masters looked at each face of his remaining deputies in turn before holding out his empty glass again to Starkey. He smiled.

'Killing that bastard would be a pleasure, Boston Bill. A real pleasure!'

ELEVEN

The dim light from the bakery window had drawn Valko like a moth to a naked flame until he was standing beside it once again. The scent of freshly baked bread filled the young outlaw with memories of a brief interlude in his violent life. A time when, in the arms of the only woman who had ever meant anything to him, he had managed to forget those who chased him. His eyes stared at the window and he wondered whether Mary White might be in there, baking bread as she had been doing when he first encountered her.

His head dropped and he realized that the rain had at last stopped beating down. He glanced back along the street as though wondering whether the curious Marshal Fallen was still watching him.

A cold shiver traced his spine and he shook. He began to wonder who had shot at him. Who else apart from Clem Everett knew that he had headed here? Then he recalled Lars Olsen and knew that the big man might have told a hundred people of their last meeting without realizing the danger it might bring to a man with a bounty on his head. How many others had Lars told about Mary being in War Smoke?

His hand stretched out, he gripped the door handle and turned it. The door was not locked. He entered and felt the heat from the ovens as an elderly man and woman toiled at making enough bread to sustain the needs of War Smoke's population for another day.

For nearly a minute Valko stood beside the open doorway before he closed it behind him. To his surprise they had not noticed his presence. Then the woman turned toward him with a tray of dough in her hands. She placed it down, then touched the arm of the man who looked towards the place where the Kid stood.

Both moved across the bakery to him. They studied him as though they had expected his arrival.

'Howdy, stranger,' the man said, clapping his hands to rid them of the surplus flour.

'Can we do something for you?' the female asked.

'Didn't you hear the shooting outside earlier?' Valko asked.

'Happens every night.' The baker gestured. 'Usually

cowboys just blowing off steam. We tend to ignore it.'

The woman edged closer to the tall bedraggled stranger. 'Is there something else we can help you with, son?'

Valko did not know where to begin. He only knew that if Mary White was anywhere in War Smoke it might be a bakery. A business she had known all her days.

'I'm looking for a lady,' Valko said.

Both of them smiled. 'Ain't the kinda place you find one of those, son.'

The Kid felt awkward. 'I mean a woman. Her name's Mary. Mary White and she hails from Indian Ridge. I was led to believe she came here to War Smoke. I think she has a small boy with her. Her son.'

They both shook their heads.

'I ain't heard of her, son,' the man said with a sigh.

'Me neither,' he woman added.

Valko touched his side. It still hurt like fury. 'It was a long shot, I guess.'

'What's your name, son?' the female asked. 'In case she does show up we can tell her about you looking for her.'

The Kid placed a hand on the door handle. 'Tell her that Roy Edwards was looking for her. She'll know who I am.'

They again nodded together as one.

'We'll tell her, Mr Edwards,' the woman said with a sigh.

'Sorry to have troubled you.' Valko opened the door and went out into the street. The baker closed the door and looked at his wife. She looked away and walked back to the tray of dough.

'I don't like lying, Bessie,' the man said as he moved behind her towards the ovens. 'Even for Mary. It ain't right.'

The woman looked at her husband. There was a tear in her eye.

'We promised her, Jeb. Mary said that a young man calling himself Roy Edwards might come looking for her. She told us to say we had never heard of her.'

The man opened the oven doors and stepped back as the heat overwhelmed him. He looked at her again.

'I know what Mary said but it don't sit well in my craw, Bessie. He ought to know the truth.'

Bessie went to the side of her man and held on to his arm as his eyes drifted heavenward. 'If he's who she said he is then the truth ain't gonna do him no good. He can't look after the boy. Mary knew that.'

'It still ain't right, Bessie girl,' the baker said. 'It just ain't right. He's that young 'un's father.'

'He's also the Valko Kid. Bounty hunters are after him all the time. Think about it. Mary knew that.'

The troubled baker nodded but still felt no better. 'Mary's the only person in this whole world I've ever lied for and that's a fact.'

'I know, Jeb.' She patted his arm and wiped her tears away. 'But think of the boy.'

The man grabbed a thick cloth, reached into the hot oven and pulled out a tray. He placed it on a work bench. His eyes stared at the golden-brown crusty loaves of bread before him.

'But, Bessie. That young man out there is gonna be chasing rainbows without ever knowing the truth.' The baker looked sickened by the deception. 'Mary had no right to make us promise to lie for her.'

'We did promise her, though,' Bessie said firmly. 'Mary loved that man with all her heart and this was her way of protecting him from the truth. And of protecting his son.'

'But a man deserves to know the truth.'

'Not when that truth will destroy him.'

The man looked at the closed door and sighed heavily.

'I ain't never pitied an outlaw before but I sure pity the Valko Kid, Bessie girl. I sure pity him.'

She gave a hushed sound and waved a finger before her lips. 'You mean Mr Edwards, Jeb. You pity Mr Roy Edwards.'

The baker lifted a tray of dough, pushed it into the oven and closed its door. He nodded to his wife.

'My mistake, Bessie. I pity Mr Edwards.'

Black Jasper Tooley had led his mount halfway across

War Smoke to the address he had memorized. Now he stood on the muddy road looking at the large house standing twenty feet away from him. He looped his reins around a cast-iron lamppost and knotted them securely before checking his Remington. He knew that sometimes even those who wished to hire him got nervous and started shooting when they saw the unexpected apparition.

The thunder still rumbled off in the distance and the rain had stopped but none of that meant anything to the gruesome figure who walked up the slight slope towards the well-appointed building. Only one thing occupied the mind of the bounty hunter and that was the reason why he was in War Smoke.

He wanted to kill the Valko Kid and anyone else who tried to interfere. That meant he needed the help of one of the town's most influential men to keep Fallen off his broad shoulders. As he strode across the ground he recalled the vague letter he had received a while back from the man who resided in the house in front of him. It seemed that there were many business folks in War Smoke who resented the fact that their marshal was honest. He had long since forgotten the details of that letter but its essence still remained burned into Tooley's memory.

These highly respected rich people wanted Fallen dead.

The seasoned bounty hunter knew that he could and would get everything he wanted if he simply played them at their own game.

He had reached barely halfway between his steaming horse and the house when he saw a drape move in one of the ground-floor windows. Tooley gripped the handle of his gun and kept on walking. Within seconds the large door opened and a man stood in its frame, holding a shotgun in his hands.

'Stop there,' the voice demanded. 'Who are you?'

Tooley did not stop but tilted his head backward and grinned at the man with the deadly weapon in his shaking hands.

'I'm the varmint ya sent for, Brent.'

Marcus Brent stepped out from the safety of his home and squinted across the well-tended gardens at the man who moved like and looked like a bear.

'Tooley? I wrote to you months back.'

The bounty hunter gave out a guttural laugh. He then closed in on the nervous owner of the town's best and most prosperous saloons.

'Ya sent for me and I come, Brent. Ya letter took a while to reach me,' Tooley joked as he pushed his way beyond the man with the double-barrelled weapon and entered the house. He paused in the lobby and removed his hat. His eyes widened as he took in the splendour of Brent's home. So this was what money could buy even crooked men, he

110

thought. He heard the door being closed behind him. He did not turn.

'I could have shot you,' Brent snarled.

'Ya still might,' Tooley grunted, 'the way that finger of yours is shaking on them triggers.'

'At least you had the brains to call when it's dark.'

'Ya got a real big house here, Brent,' Tooley remarked, a tone of envy in his gruff voice. 'Must be a lotta money in owning saloons in these parts.'

Brent kept the shotgun in his hands as he led the way to his library. Books filled every shelf from floor to ceiling. He heard the footsteps of the large man behind him. The saloon owner sat down next to the window from where he had noticed Tooley's arrival and rested the weapon on his desk. Its barrels were still aimed at the bounty hunter.

Tooley moved slowly but with purpose. He kept staring at all the books which filled every inch of space on the rooms four walls. Then he sat down opposite Brent.

'Ya like reading?'

Brent nodded.

'Strange!' Tooley laughed. 'I always found all a man needs is to be able to read wanted posters.'

Marcus Brent leaned over his shotgun and looked at the face of the man he had sent for months earlier.

'You took a long time to get here, Tooley.'

'I've bin moving around after vermin,' the burly

man explained. 'Rats don't come to you. Ya gotta go after them.'

'I thought that you might not wish to accept the job I proposed to you.' Brent pointed to a decanter of whiskey on the desk. He watched his guest lift the glass vessel and pull its stopper.

Tooley grinned until most of his remaining blackened teeth showed. 'Never give that job a second thought, Brent. I'm here to kill the Valko Kid.'

'But my proposal would pay you equally well.' Brent swallowed hard as he watched the bounty hunter start to drink from the decanter.

'Ya figure?' Tooley looked as though he did not believe his host. 'Valko's worth twenty-five grand.'

'Yes, I know he is,' Brent said. 'My offer was for you to dispose of the marshal because he's become a nuisance to my business. Not just mine but half the other businesses in town have also been suffering. Fallen follows the law too close to the letter and that cramps profits.'

Tooley lowered the decanter from his lips. Whiskey dribbled down from the mouth of the bearded man. He closed one eye and stared hard at the saloon owner.

'Ya wants Fallen killed. Simple to say but mighty darn hard to do. That lawman is fast and real lucky.'

'Are you scared?' Brent asked. His index finger curled round the triggers of his hefty weapon in case

112

he had to defend himself against the big man's anger.

'Nope.' Tooley took another long drink, then paused for the fumes to subside from his lungs. 'I just reckon that that lawman is hard to kill. I heard that a lotta folks have tried and not one of them has lived to celebrate. Fallen and me had a run-in once, as ya recall. I almost got lynched.'

'As I said, I am not alone in wanting Fallen killed.' Brent sighed nervously. 'I have many partners in this plan and we are sharing the cost. I dare say we could double our original fee.'

The bounty hunter straightened up. He rested the decanter on his left knee and stared through the lamplight at Brent.

'Ya reckon ya got that kinda money? Fifty thousand dollars? I never thought there was that much money in the whole territory.'

'There is,' Brent confirmed. 'And it's all yours if you do this simple thing for my partners and me. It would take months for War Smoke to get another marshal and in that time my friends and I could prosper.'

Tooley leaned forward and looked at the floor. He had originally thought of using Brent to get the town council to send the troublesome marshal on a long journey so that he could achieve his goal of killing Valko and whoever else got in his way without facing any legal charges. It had only been a well-bribed jury that had prevented him from being hanged for killing three innocent townsfolk as well as a wanted outlaw the last time he had encountered Fallen.

It was a situation he did not wish to be repeated.

Tooley mulled over the proposition carefully and then looked through his bushy eyebrows at Brent. He knew that if he killed Fallen he did not have to worry himself about how he went about killing Valko. It all seemed too sweet.

'All I gotta do to earn that money is kill Fallen. Right?'

Brent smiled.

'Right, Tooley.'

'When do I get paid?'

'On completion of the task.'

'Huh?'

'When you have killed Fallen.'

Black Jasper stood, finished what was left of the whiskey and placed the empty decanter down on the desk. He surveyed the room again, then turned on his heels.

'Right.'

As the bounty hunter reached the door, Brent called out.

'When?'

Tooley looked over his shoulder. It was a frighten-ing sight which most men only saw a few moments before the bounty hunter sent them to their Maker.

'Before sunup suit ya?'

Marcus Brent clasped his hands as if in prayer. 'That would suit me real fine, Tooley.'

The large man in the fur coat laughed out loud and resumed his walk to the front door. The sound of it being slammed shut behind him echoed around the large house as Brent gave out a muffled laugh.

'Yes!' he said.

TWELVE

Marshal Matt Fallen had no reason to know it but there were six ruthless gunmen in town who would attempt to end his life before dawn ever reached War Smoke. Their guns were going to make him a target this night. With the gold of powerful men in their pockets they would try to earn their blood money as quickly as they could. Many had tried and failed over the years. It was a price which had to be paid by those like Fallen. Men who were like oak trees and refused to bend into the jaws of corruption. Men who obeyed the laws of the land however bitter the taste could often be.

The marshal's office was still bathed in the amber glowing light of its solitary coal-tar lamp. There were still a few hours of darkness remaining before a new day showed itself. With darkness came shadow and where there were shadows there was danger. Somehow the marshal had always been able to sense when danger was close. His survival instincts were still honed like a straight razor.

Fallen seldom used a Winchester or any other sort of weapon apart from his trusty seven-inch barrelled Colt. Yet for some reason he silently unlocked the chain which held the office's rifles on the wall rack and lifted one from its perch. He ran a hand along its length and nodded.

'I see you cleaned these rifles like I told you, Elmer,' the tall man said to his deputy.

Elmer nodded. 'I oiled and loaded the whole bunch of them.'

'Good.' Fallen tossed one of the rifles to his underling and then pulled another from the rack for himself. He cranked its mechanism and, satisfied that the weapon was in perfect order, he pulled the hand guard back up to shield the trigger.

The younger man stood with the Winchester in his hands. He looked curious as he walked to the side of the marshal. 'Well, tickle me pink. Ya never uses rifles, Marshal Fallen. How come ya plucking us a couple off the wall tonight?'

'Don't you remember that varmint earlier?'

'The one who tried to kill that drummer?'

'Yep. He was using a Winchester and if he's still in town I don't want him opening up on us when we're only packing six-shooters, Elmer.' Fallen rested the barrel of the rifle against his left shoulder. 'A man could get himself killed for lack of range.'

'And rifles got range enough to spare.' The deputy sighed.

Fallen walked to the window and stared out into the dark street. Storefronts had been getting darker for the previous couple of hours as one after another the businesses closed for the night. He rested an elbow on the brass drape-rail and kept on studying Front Street.

'You ever get a feeling in your craw that something's brewing, Elmer? Some kinda trouble you can't pin down but you seem to feel it in your innards. Do you?'

The deputy knew they were getting close to the time when they did their rounds of the numerous streets and alleyways which made up War Smoke. He rubbed his flat belly.

'The only feeling in my guts is 'coz I'm mighty hungry.'

Fallen glanced out along the street in the direction of the café. Its lights were no longer cascading out into Front Street. The marshal turned and glanced at the office wall clock. 'Looks like the café shut early tonight. Must have bin the storm sent them home earlier than usual, Elmer.'

The deputy looked upset as he hurried to the marshal's side and looked out to the café. 'No! If that don't beat all! I missed my dinner and now I'm gonna miss my supper.'

Fallen moved away from the window. 'We've bin busy.'

'I'm still hungry though, Marshal Fallen. Powerful hungry and that ain't no lie.'

The marshal opened the door and led the way out into the street. He looked up at the stars which were now starting to show themselves between the departing black clouds.

'I'm a tad hungry myself. We could try and catch us a bowl of chilli when we get to the east side of town. That little Mexican cantina never closes its doors.' Fallen locked the office door behind them and began to walk. 'How would that suit you, Elmer?'

'Them Mexicans don't close their door coz they ain't got no damn door, Marshal Fallen.' Elmer piped up as he trailed the broad-shouldered man. 'Some cowboy roped and rode off with it last month. Anyways, it's a tad late for chilli, ain't it?'

'My treat.'

'Well if ya paying I reckon I could force a bowl or two down.' The deputy did a shuffle until he was keeping pace with the marshal. 'I just hope I last to breakfast on Mexican vittles though.'

'Can you keep alert, Elmer?'

'I guess so,' the deputy answered. 'Why?'

'In case someone tries to shoot us.'

The pair of rifle-toting lawmen continued on their regular route into Trail Street.

They were well-fuelled by Boston Bill Starkey's whiskey and each had a fifty-dollar gold piece in his pocket. The men had no idea that this was probably as close as any of them would ever get to the $1,000 Starkey had offered them. For men like Fallen were not easily killed, however many guns were trained upon his large frame. The five men who wore tin stars moved out from the brightly illuminated gambling-hall with their guns ready for killing. Sheriff Masters stopped on the boardwalk and looked down the street to where a lantern hung on a hook outside the marshal's office. He grinned widely. He believed that there would soon be a vacancy in that office and he would be more than willing to take it. He huddled in the middle of his four men and checked his six-shooters with drunken hands.

'There's a light on in the marshal's office, Sheriff,' Withers said, pointing across the street. 'They must still be in there.'

'That Fallen is gonna rue the day he messed with us, boys,' Masters declared. 'He'll learn it don't pay to step on another lawman's toes.'

'I'll enjoy filling him with lead, Sheriff,' Withers said, snorting.

'How we gonna do this, Sheriff?' Cooper asked eagerly.

Withers, Davis and Kent leaned closer to the man who was no more sober than they were themselves, as if his slurred words might somehow enlighten them.

Masters pushed one of his guns into its holster and nodded to himself as, somewhat breathless, he forced his way to the edge of the boardwalk. He leaned against a porch upright and stared along the street as his thumb pulled back on the gun hammer. The town was reasonably quiet after the storm and only a few riders had ventured out. His eyes studied the muddy street, then he spotted a few barrels outside the closed and shuttered hardware store.

Masters pointed the barrel of his weapon at the store. 'I figure some of us will head over there and push them barrels away from the store front. A clean view of the marshal's office from there right enough. Yep.'

'Good place to ambush that damned marshal.' Trey Withers chuckled knowingly. 'As soon as he shows his face outside that office we'll cut him to ribbons. Right?'

'Right,' Masters agreed. 'They gotta come out of there sometime soon and when they do we'll be waiting for them.'

'I didn't know that if ya was a member of a posse ya could kill other lawmen, Sheriff,' Davis said.

The sheriff managed to straighten up. He rubbed his chin thoughtfully. 'Where do ya reckon the rest of us ought to be if'n we want to get that Fallen caught in a crossfire?'

Cy Kent staggered to the side of the sheriff and pointed a finger in the direction of the barber shop.

'I think that Casey's over yonder looks a damn good place for one man to shoot from,' he suggested.

'Behind the water trough?' Masters asked.

Kent nodded hard. 'Yep.'

'Good thinking, Cy.'

The sheriff began to walk along the boardwalk. His eyes kept looking at the muddy ground between their side of the street and where the marshal's office stood.

'Take ya places, men,' Masters ordered. 'We got us a thousand dollars to earn.'

The drunken quartet of deputies moved to their chosen places and readied their weapons.

Valko had been standing in his bare feet in the hotel room for nearly ten minutes, staring at his ruined clothes on the floor, when he decided that there was no alternative. If he wanted to venture out and go and check on his friend Clem's health he had to open the canvas bag and put on his trail gear. He opened the bag and stared at the black pants and shirt before pulling them free. As he climbed into the clothes which had become the trademark of his infamy his eyes looked at the folded gunbelt and his pair of Colt .45s in the hand-tooled holsters. He lifted them up and swung them around his slender hips. He buckled them and then reached down to tie the leather laces around his thighs. The Kid was still hurting from the stitches in his side but that seemed to fade into a distant place in his confused mind as he retrieved his boots from the bottom of the bag and pulled them on to his bare feet.

He kept thinking about the elderly couple in the bakery. They had looked honest enough, he thought. But there had been something in their voices which troubled the outlaw.

He walked to the window and pulled its lace curtain aside. He stared down into the street. People were now walking around as the storm became little more than a memory.

Valko rested a hand on the grip of his left gun and took a deep breath. He knew that there were a thousand reasons why he might never discover the truth about the woman who had never faded from his thoughts. She might have been ill, as some in Indian Ridge had said, or there might have been another reason for her leaving the town where she had spent her entire life.

The child deserved better than being branded for something which was beyond his comprehension. Maybe Mary had left the distant town to give the boy a chance of a normal life.

Could that be it?

Valko was about to release his hold on the curtain when he saw someone he recognized riding slowly along below the light of a streetlamp. His heart suddenly began to pound.

There was no mistaking the bounty hunter whose range he had managed to keep out of for ten years or more.

'Tooley,' he muttered to himself. 'Black Jasper!'

Valko's hand tightened on the grip of his weapon as a bead of sweat trailed down his face. He dropped the lace drape and stepped back into the room. Only the edge of the bed stopped his retreat from the window.

'What's he doing here?'

The outlaw rubbed his face. He knew that Black Jasper never wasted a mile riding in his pursuit of men with bounties he wanted to claim. Like so many of his breed, the bounty hunter always went for men wanted dead or alive. He never took prisoners.

It was not his way.

If Tooley was in War Smoke he was here for a reason and that reason was to kill someone with a handsome reward on his head.

The bounty hunter was here to kill *him*.

The young man picked up the bag and dragged out his battered Stetson. The bag was now empty. He cast it across the room against the wall.

A million thoughts exploded inside his skull as he beat the hat into shape and placed it upon his head. Somehow Tooley knew that the Valko Kid was in War Smoke. That would have brought him here all right. There was no way he would pass up a $25,000 reward. Not Black Jasper. Even a vague hint of such a bounty would bring him riding a hundred miles or more. Riding in with his tongue hanging out of his mouth.

Valko gritted his teeth.

He grabbed the door handle and rushed out into the hall. He walked to the back stairs and descended them two at a time until he reached the hotel's rear door. Valko walked out into the cool air and darkness, then started along the back alley he knew would take him behind every building on the opposite side of Front Street to where Doc Weaver's office stood.

The clouds were starting to thin above him. Moonlight was beginning to reach the sprawling town but so far none of its eerie light had found the alley.

As Valko increased his pace he tried to think.

Tooley had to know that the Valko Kid was in War Smoke, the outlaw silently told himself. That killer bought and sold information about wanted men in every town west of the Pecos.

It was no coincidence that he was here.

Tooley wanted Valko.

Like a hunter wants the head of a stag on his wall, Tooley wanted the ultimate prize of being the man who bettered the legendary Valko.

That had to be it.

The young man reached a wall, leapt over it and carried on his hectic pace. Valko knew that his naïve idea of meeting Mary White again and things being as simple as they had once been was little more than a deluded pipe dream.

Men with hefty bounties on them had to keep on running from men like Tooley. Even from men like Matt Fallen.

The Kid reached a corner and turned up the small street which led close to the livery. He could smell the horses and then he thought about Snow.

That stallion could carry him away from anything Tooley rode, he thought. The Kid turned down another narrow street, then stopped when he saw the tall newly built livery stable straight ahead of him. He paused and looked at it for what felt like a lifetime. The building was so new its wood still had sap oozing from its boards. Not even a lick of paint had been brushed across it.

Valko was torn between staying to see how his pal was and going into the stable, taking his horse and fleeing whilst darkness could still give him a little cover. He began to walk to the livery when he thought about his brave friend again.

Clem Everett was still at Doc Weaver's.

Still close to death – or maybe actually dead.

The Kid hestitated.

He placed a hand on a fence wall and lowered his head. It was bad enough being innocent and branded a killer but he had never allowed himself to act like a cowardly outlaw.

Every instinct told him to get Snow, saddle up and ride, but he could never just run out on his friend. Clem was his only real friend. He looked at the ground. The moonlight was now illuminating the narrow confines of the street where he stood. A street which not only led to the livery but to Front Street.

Valko knew the old man would never desert him, however dangerous the situation became.

The Kid watched his feet turn and start back towards the main thoroughfare of War Smoke. He knew that he was probably heading for his own death if Black Jasper Tooley spotted him but he kept on walking. Then another thought came to him. Dressed as he now was Fallen would know his suspicions were correct: Mr Edwards was in fact the Valko Kid.

Would Fallen be the one to kill him?

Each step seemed to bring him into even more moonlight as more clouds disappeared from the sky above him. Valko walked on and knew that if he were honest with himself he did not truly care if his days of running ended here in this remote settlement.

He had lost heart.

Mary had long gone, he told himself. Gone with their son to find a better place where the stain of the Valko Kid could never harm either of them again.

What if it did end here?

War Smoke was as good or bad a town as every other town he had visited over the years he had been running from the law. His flight had to end somewhere.

Maybe it would be best for Mary and the son he knew he would never meet if this was where the story finished.

Then he considered the events which had occurred earlier.

Valko thought about the bounty hunter again and nodded as he walked. It must have been Tooley who had shot him.

That evil hunter of two-legged prey was one of the best at his profession. Only Tooley could have spotted an outlaw even when he was dressed like a drummer. Tooley was also loco enough to open up with his rifle even if it was not an outlaw he was shooting at. Tooley had killed as many innocent folks as he had killed outlaws in his time.

The famed outlaw flicked off his leather safety loops from his gun hammers and rested his hands upon the grips. He was getting closer to the street.

Front Street was now less than ten paces away. Whatever happened now was in the lap of the gods.

Valko looked up at the sky. The large moon mocked his attempts to move unseen to the doctor's office. A thousand stars only added to his misery.

It was too light. Too damn light.

Now even the moon was betraying him.

The Valko Kid could see Doc Weaver's office across the muddy street. Its lamplight glowed behind the lowered blind and for the briefest of moments made the outlaw forget his fears. He stepped out from the narrow alley and began to cross the muddy street toward the place where he knew Clem Everett lay.

The slim young man clad entirely in black had only taken three steps toward his destination when all hell broke loose.

Colby Masters' raised voice cut through the silence like a meat cleaver. 'That's the Valko Kid, boys. Kill the varmint. Kill him. That *hombre*'s worth a fortune.'

His depraved followers did not require telling twice.

Suddenly it was as though the storm had returned. The deafening gunfire exploded from both sides of the Kid as he reached Front Street. Only shadows gave the wanted outlaw any protection on the side of the street where the moonlight failed to play.

Blistering volleys of lead tore from each side. To

Valko's left, Kent and Cooper unleashed their six-shooters' lethal fury as soon as they spotted the Kid walking towards the doctor's office. To the outlaw's right Withers and Davis, who were kneeling beside Masters behind the barrels outside the hardware store, saw the red tapers of bullets cut across their field of vision. They obeyed the sheriff and also started fanning their gun hammers.

Sheriff Masters hauled both his guns from their leather resting places and cocked hammers. Like a man desperate to achieve an ambition he had begun to think had eluded him, Masters blasted his guns blindly.

Valko twisted and turned as the nearest porch upright shattered into a million fiery splinters when a score of bullets tore into it. Burning fragments of the wooden four-by-four showered over the outlaw. Knowing that he had been caught in a crossfire, Valko threw himself on to his belly in the mud of the street. Faster than any of his attackers thought possible he turned on to his back and pulled both his matched Colts from their holsters.

The Kid looked to both sides as lead kicked up the mud all around his prostrate body.

He could see the plumes of gunsmoke and red poison spewing from their gun barrels and began to retaliate. Few men could have matched the prowess of the outlaw who lay firing to both sides with quick turns of his head to locate his targets. At first Valko's shots merely kept them down, then his aim became more precise.

Josh Cooper was first to feel the venom of the Kid's deadly accurate bullets. He was knocked off his feet by the sheer force of the bullet and flew the short distance to the front of Casey's barber shop window. Cy Kent ducked when he saw and heard Cooper smashing through the large pane. Glass shattered all over the boardwalk. Kent gulped as his eyes saw Cooper's body go limp as it hung on the edge of the wooden sill. A large jagged chunk of glass had gone straight through the dead man's torso. It pinned him to the spot where he had landed.

Blood flowed down the front of the store and did not stop even when it encircled Kent's knees.

'Sheriff Masters,' Kent screamed out hysterically as he kept firing to where the Kid lay. 'Josh's dead. What'll I do? Sheriff! Answer me!'

Masters did not answer. He just continued firing into the dark, smoke-filled street. It did not matter to him if he lost all his men as long as he achieved his goal and killed the man with the huge bounty on his head.

Valko turned on to his knees as even more bullets came at him from both sides of the street. He could feel their heat as they passed close.

Too damn close.

Then as Masters made to move away from the barrels he saw a red shaft of light cut through the air next to his left arm. It was another of Valko's bullets. His head turned as if to follow the bullet's path and as he did so he was covered in Bo Davis's gore. Davis had been hit right between the eyes and what had been inside his skull suddenly cannonaded over the stunned sheriff and Withers.

There was nothing more sickening than the feel of another man's warm brains on your own flesh. Frantically Masters tried to wipe the mess off his face with his sleeves as his hands still clung to his guns.

'This ain't going the way we planned,' Withers yelled at the man beside him.

'Then kill that bastard,' Masters shrieked.

The sight of death so close sobered up Masters faster than a lake of black coffee. He fell on to his knees and shook the brass casings from his smoking guns.

'Bo and Josh are dead, Sheriff,' Withers screamed in disbelief.

'We'll all be dead if'n we don't kill that damn outlaw,' the sheriff yelled back as his fingers fumbled for fresh bullets on his belt and forced them into his weapons' chambers. 'Keep shooting! Kill Valko! Kill him or he'll kill us! There ain't no third way, Trey.'

Reluctantly Withers eased around and, hiding behind the barrel, he tried to do as Masters ordered.

He now felt that their perfect place to ambush someone from had become little more than a trap. A trap he knew he would never escape from.

Thick gunsmoke hung in the shadows between the hardware store and the outlaw. Using it as a shield the Kid ran back to the relative safety of a water trough. Then he felt a bullet as it cut past his right wrist and took the skin off the top of his hand.

He swung on his knees and fanned his gun hammer.

Cy Kent shook as the shot caught him dead centre. He tried to rise, then tumbled off the boardwalk and landed head first in the soft mud.

Kent did not move again.

Now the shooting was only coming from one side, Valko told himself as he quickly reloaded his guns and crouched beside the trough. The bullets soon found his new hiding-place and he could feel the water-filled trough rocking against his back as one bullet after another hit it. Jets of water showered over him as he closed the chambers of his Colts in turn and cocked their hammers again.

The Kid had no idea how many of his attackers were left. All he was certain about was that they kept on shooting at him. They had him pinned down.

Around the corner in Trail Street, Fallen swung full circle and aimed his rifle back at Front Street as the ear-splitting echoes of the gunshots rang out all around them. Elmer cocked his Winchester and ran to the side of the marshal. Both men were stunned and shocked. Neither knew who was firing and what the target might be. The deputy swallowed hard and tried to work out what was happening. He looked at his tall companion.

'Marshal?' His voice begged for answers.

Fallen gritted his teeth. 'C'mon!' he yelled.

Both lawmen raced along Trail Street with their rifles ready in their hands. As the marshal reached the corner he could see the bullets exploding from two separate places halfway down the long, wide thoroughfare.

'There,' Fallen said pointing his rifle.

Elmer paused beside Fallen. 'Who in tarnation is doing all that shooting, Marshal Fallen?'

'Damned if I know, Elmer,' the marshal answered grimly. 'But I'm gonna find out pretty damn quick. C'mon!'

The deputy had to run faster than he had ever run before just to keep up with the tall lawman. They had just cleared the café's façade when suddenly the moonlight danced along the barrels of the guns in the hands of Masters and his cohort Withers.

'See them?'

'I surely do.'

Then the guns were turned away from the outlaw and began to fire at Fallen and his deputy. Venomous lead came at them through clouds of gunsmoke. Fallen threw himself down on the boardwalk as his loyal companion leapt off the boardwalk into the muddy street. Elmer rolled over until half his body was under the boardwalk behind a water trough.

'Who is that shooting at us, Marshal Fallen?'

'If I knew that I'd be a lot happier than I am right now, Elmer.' Fallen crawled with the rifle jutting out before him and then saw the moonlight catch the tin star on Master's chest. 'I don't believe it, Elmer!'

'What?' the deputy asked.

'That's the back-shooting sheriff we ran into up in the rocks a few hours back,' Fallen snarled.

'What's he doing shooting up War Smoke?'

'Probably the same reason him and his cronies shot old Clem Everett,' Fallen spat as he kept on crawling. 'I figure they've seen us.'

'Tell them who we are, Marshal Fallen,' Elmer suggested. 'We surely don't want them to shoot us by mistake.'

Fallen saw the lead tapers pass over his head and knew that he could not rise. He continued to crawl until he was beside a wooden upright. It was a mighty thin upright to give cover to a mighty broad-shouldered man. Even if that man was on his belly.

'I'm ordering you to quit that shooting, Masters,' Fallen called out loudly. 'This is Marshal Fallen.'

Masters edged along to stand beside Withers and

grinned at the troubled man with the smoking guns in his trembling hands.

'This'll be a real big payday for us if we can finish both of them off, Trey. Fallen and Valko! We'll be set for the rest of our lives.'

Trey Withers tried to swallow. It was impossible. He had no spittle.

Just at that moment the door to Doc Weaver's office opened wide and the medical man stepped out into the moonlight. He looked angry as he shook his fist at the air.

'Will you quit shooting? I got me a sick man in here!'

Valko raised his head above the edge of the bullet-scarred trough and saw the guns of Masters and Withers appear from above the barrels outside the hardware store. They were trained upon the elderly doctor.

Defying his own fear, Valko holstered his guns, jolted to his feet and ran across the street towards Doc. Just as he reached the boardwalk he heard the sound of guns explode into action behind him. He leapt like a puma, caught Doc around the middle. Both men went flying into the office as bullets tore the doorframe apart.

Doc lay winded for a few seconds as Valko jumped to his feet and pulled his guns free of their holsters once more.

'How's Clem, Doc?' the Kid asked as he leaned against the door and squinted out into the moonlight.

Still flat on his back, Doc Weaver slowly raised his head and wheezed. 'He'll be OK, Mr Edwards. I ain't too sure about me though.'

THIRTEEN

A mere few seconds after firing at Valko and Doc the guns of Masters and Withers returned their fury back on Fallen and his deputy. Bullets tore even more of the side of the café wall apart, keeping the marshal and his friend pinned down. Smouldering debris showered over both lawmen as the onslaught persisted. Fallen fired his rifle back along the street at the barrels.

'Damn it all. I got the range but I can't get a clean shot,' Fallen snarled.

'Maybe I could get closer, Marshal Fallen,' Elmer suggested. 'I could crawl out across the street and try and get me an angle to fire from.'

'Stay right where you are.' Fallen rolled off the boardwalk and landed next to his deputy in the still-soft mud. Both men tried to make out what was going on but neither could see clearly through the clouds of acrid smoke which hung on the cool night air. The marshal propped himself up slightly and cupped his mouth with the palm of his left hand.

'Quit shooting,' Fallen boomed out. 'This is Marshal Fallen and I'm getting mighty angry at being shot at.'

The shooting stopped for a few seconds.

'Ya figure we can stand up now, Marshal Fallen?' Elmer asked innocently. 'Ya done told them who we was and all.'

Fallen continued to stare along the long street. His curiosity had been aroused.

'Why'd they start shooting in a different direction a couple of minutes back, Elmer? And what were they shooting at?'

Elmer opened his mouth but when his brain failed to reach an answer he simply closed it again.

Fallen eased forward close to a hitching rail. 'Can you make out anything down there, Elmer?'

The deputy screwed up his eyes. 'The gunsmoke is pretty darn dense but it sure looks like Doc's door is open to me.'

Suddenly both lawmen flinched when Masters and Withers opened up with another volley of shots aimed at the front of the doctor's office and home. The sound of wood being riddled with bullets rang out along Front Street.

'They are shooting at Doc's!' Fallen gasped in

bewildered surprise. 'But why?'

'Maybe that posse thinks the real Valko is in there and not old Clem Everett,' Elmer suggested.

'This is plumb loco,' Fallen spat out.

More shots rang out. This time they were again aimed at the front of Doc's office. Fallen squinted hard, then saw someone inside the office firing back at the men hidden by the hardware store. The shots were well grouped and for a moment neither Masters nor Withers could respond.

'That can't be Doc firing,' Fallen said knowingly. 'Whoever is in there with him can shoot and shoot well.'

Elmer crawled through the mud behind the prostrate figure of his superior and cranked his rifle again. Fallen raised himself up on an elbow to get a better view from their low vantage point.

'Maybe the varmint who shot at that Edwards fella is wanted and that posse got him pinned down inside Doc's place?' The deputy was now clutching at straws in order to try and make sense of the battlefield they had stumbled into.

'I surely doubt that, Elmer. Seems to me that there must be something mighty valuable to them inside Doc's,' Fallen said.

'What?'

'Who,' Fallen corrected.

'Huh?' The deputy tilted his head as he crawled

next to the slowly advancing marshal. 'Are ya talking in riddles now? I ain't in no mood for no riddles. I'm still powerful hungry and them critters are keeping me from my supper. Even if it was only a bowl of chilli.'

'What if the real Valko Kid is in there?' the marshal proposed. 'He finds out his pal has been wounded and taken to Doc's. That Sheriff Masters and his cronies found out and have him cornered. Could be.'

'Maybe,' Elmer conceded.

Fallen touched his friend's arm. 'Hush up now. I'm gonna try something.'

As more shots blasted the front of Doc's office apart, the deputy watched as the marshal carefully got to his feet using the hitching rail for support. Then Fallen carefully stepped back up on to the boardwalk. Unseen he moved close to the wall and used the café's doorframe to shield his body. Fallen took off his coat and balanced it on the barrel of his Winchester before removing his Stetson and placing that over the neck of his jacket. The lawman took a deep breath, then called out again as loudly as he could manage as he held the rifle at arm's length.

'This is Fallen. Give yourself up, Masters.'

No sooner had he finished his declaration than Masters and Withers opened up. Their gunfire ripped the rifle from his hand and tore his hat and coat to shreds.

'Are ya OK, Marshal Fallen?' Elmer whispered.

Fallen looked at the startled Elmer who was watching from the edge of the boardwalk.

'That's curious,' the marshal said, pulling his Colt from his holster. 'I think they want to kill me as bad as whoever they got pinned down over yonder.'

'I reckon they meant to kill ya, Marshal Fallen,' Elmer said with a nod. 'That sure couldn't have bin an accident. Ya told 'em who ya was clear enough.'

Fallen held his gun against his chest. 'Stay there and give me plenty of cover with that rifle of yours. OK?'

Elmer got on to his knees, raised the Winchester to his shoulder and closed one eye as he looked along its length.

'I'm ready. Gimme the word and I'll start to shoot, Marshal Fallen.'

'Now!' Fallen yelled. He started to run down the boardwalk towards the hardware store and the two men crouching in front of its façade. Each long stride was matched by a bullet from Elmer's rifle as he attempted to keep the men behind the barrels pinned down.

No raging bull could have matched Fallen's snorting as he pounded along the boards with his gun held out before him, ready to fire at anyone who poked their head above the barrels.

Masters blinked hard when he saw the unmistakable figure of the tall Fallen racing towards them. He had thought that he and his cohort had already finished the marshal. Frantically he punched Withers in the shoulder and pointed at the charging lawman, who was getting closer with every beat of his pounding heart.

'Fallen!' Masters managed to say before he turned and cocked the hammers of both his pistols in turn. 'He ain't dead! He's coming!'

'What the hell?' Trey Withers spun on his rump and clawed at his own hammers as he too saw the large figure bearing down on them.

Both men went to rise as Elmer's aim improved and rocked the barrels before them. Masters leaned to his left and blasted at the marshal a fraction of a second before the tall man flew over the barrels and caught both men around the throats with his powerful outstretched arms.

The sheer force knocked both men flat. Weapons flew from their hands. Fallen rolled head over heels and landed on his boots. He turned far faster than a man of his build should ever have been able to turn. His eyes searched the shadows for his Colt, then saw it a few feet from where Masters' own guns lay. He made to move when the dazed Withers shook his head and grabbed hold of the nearest gun. He turned and was about to fire when another rifle shot rang out from Elmer's Winchester. A scream rang out along Front Street. Withers arched and fell on to his face. The gun flew from his lifeless hand and slid across the weathered boards towards the marshal.

Masters groaned and stared through bloody eyebrows at the man who had bettered him. Then a twisted snarl etched the face of the sheriff.

'Ya nothing, Fallen. Nothing at all. I'm the man that'll kill ya and take ya job.'

'This town don't like vermin, Masters,' Fallen replied in a low deep drawl. 'Not even if they wear stars.'

'That must be why nobody likes you.'

The marshal was crouching and looking at the guns waiting on the boards to be claimed by whichever of them was the quicker to reach them.

Both men hovered.

Both men leapt at the guns. Fallen jumped across the distance between them to grab at his seven-inch-barrelled Colt at the same moment that Masters threw himself full-bodied towards his own scattered weapons.

They crashed into one another. Their heads butted together like mountain goats.

A dazed Fallen saw Masters' hands manage to snatch up one of the guns. He grabbed both the sheriff's wrists and used his superior strength to twist

Masters' hands back. But Masters defied his own agony and held on to the gun as they fell across the barrels and tumbled into the muddy street. The gun fired and a cloud of blinding smoke filled Fallen's eyes. They wrestled across the soft, wet ground. The gun fired again, then Masters brought up a boot and caught Fallen in the belly. He forced the marshal off him and laughed as the bigger man went hurtling backwards.

Unable to see his foe, Fallen could only listen as he heard the gun hammer being pulled back until it fully locked into firing position.

'Beg for ya worthless life, Fallen,' Masters spat.

'The hell I'll beg a back-shooter.'

Then the deafening sound of shots rang out. Their thunder filled Front Street. Fallen buckled and staggered. As he hit the boardwalk he felt the burning in his shoulder.

But he was alive. He rubbed his eyes and through streams of burning tears saw what was left of Colby Masters lying face up in the middle of the street. Smoke rose from the barrel of the gun in the dead man's hand.

'Ya all right, Marshal Fallen?' Elmer called out as he ran through the mud with his smoking Winchester in his hands.

'Good shot, Elmer,' Fallen said as the younger man reached him. 'Ya saved my bacon there!'

Elmer cleared his throat and pointed towards Doc's where the Valko Kid stood holding his own smoking guns in his hands.

'It weren't me that saved ya,' Elmer stammered. 'I plumb run out of bullets.'

Fallen shook his head and squinted again. 'Then who did shoot that worthless lump of horseflesh, Elmer?'

'Mr Edwards did,' Elmer said. 'Or maybe it was Valko. I'm kinda confused, but he done it OK. Saw ya was helpless and he just squeezed his triggers and sent Masters off to hell.'

Matt Fallen took his deputy's arm and gave out a sigh as he felt the bullet in his own shoulder burn like a branding iron.

'Pick up my Colt, Elmer,' he said as Valko walked towards them. He looked at the wanted man through his weeping eyes and announced: 'I reckon I have to arrest that outlaw.'

Elmer stooped and plucked the long-barrelled gun off the boardwalk. He handed it to the marshal, then gasped in amazement.

'What? Ya can't go arresting him, Marshal Fallen! He done saved ya life.'

'The law's the law,' Fallen said drily.

Valko had heard every word. He holstered his guns, raised his hands and moved towards them slowly.

146

'Reckon you gotta do your job, Marshal.'

Both Fallen and Elmer were confused. The marshal looked hard at the young man with disbelieving eyes.

'You're giving up that easy?'

Valko shrugged. 'If I didn't, I'd have to kill you, Marshal. It don't make a lot of sense killing someone when you just saved their life.'

'Ain't that what the Valko Kid does?' Elmer queried his superior. 'Kill folks and all. Ya better be careful in case it's a trick.'

Fallen held his shoulder and felt the blood seeping through his fingers. 'I'm gonna let Doc look at this wound, Elmer. Then I'll fret about him tricking us.'

Elmer clutched his rifle and narrowed his eyes as he looked at Valko. 'Ya don't fool me, Valko. Saving Marshal Fallen's life was some sort of trick. One move and I'll let ya have it.'

Fallen smiled and gestured to the Kid. 'Lower them arms, Mr Edwards. Elmer ain't gonna kill anyone. Not with an empty rifle anyways.'

Just as the three figures turned towards Doc's office the sound of a horse whinnying broke the silence which had pervaded Front Street since the lethal gunplay had ceased.

Valko pointed. 'There.'

Both lawmen looked to where the Kid was pointing a finger.

The sight of Black Jasper Tooley was awesome in the daytime, but by night, when only moonlight and shadows illuminated men's darkest nightmares, he was terrifying.

All three looked at the horseman who had dragged his reins up to his chest and stopped his lathered-up mount outside the Red Dog. He sat staring at the three men with eyes which seemed to glow in the saloon's cascading lamplight.

'Howdy, Marshal!' Tooley flourished with a wave of his free hand. 'Bet ya never thought I'd come back.'

Fallen stopped with his two companions to either side of him. His gun hand still pressed against his wounded shoulder as he stepped away from both Elmer and Valko to get a better look at the horseman.

'Tooley!' He spat the name as though he had just tasted poison. 'I told you never to come back to War Smoke. You better have a damn good reason for being here.'

'Marshal Fallen.' Tooley rammed his spurs into the flesh of his horse. The creature walked towards the men bathed in the light from Doc's office. 'I have me a couple of damn good reasons for being in this dung heap.'

Fallen was about to remove his hand from his shoulder when pain racked his entire body. He gritted his teeth and knew that even if he could reach his holstered Colt the blood which clung to his fingers would make it doubtful that he could actually draw and fire his weapon.

'I'm listening out for them two good reasons, Tooley,' the marshal growled.

'I'm here to kill two men, Fallen,' the bounty hunter said in a loud joyous manner. 'Two stinking men who don't deserve to live an hour longer.'

Aware of Fallen's plight, Valko walked away from the deputy and stood next to the tall marshal. His hands hovered over the grips of his own weaponry.

'Reckon I must be one of them men you have to kill.'

Tooley pulled back on his reins. His eyes focused on the lean man clad in black with the handsome shooting rig strapped around his middle.

'If ya owns a white stallion and ya name's Valko, I reckon ya right,' the horseman grunted. 'Ya one of the varmints I'm gonna kill.'

Valko nodded. 'Any time you figure you're ready to draw that hogleg. I'll oblige you by joining in.'

'You ain't killing anyone in my town, Tooley,' Fallen said.

'Wrong, Fallen,' the bounty hunter grunted, then he laughed.

Fallen cleared his throat. 'Hold on there, Tooley. Just to ease my curiosity a tad, who is the other man in War Smoke you intend killing?'

Black Jasper started to laugh even louder. It was not the laugh of a man who had just heard a funny joke but the laugh of a man who had lost all touch with humanity. Killing had become his only reason to exist. He eyed all three men on the ground before him. Two he could easily dismiss, for one had an empty rifle in his hands and the other was wounded. Only the Valko Kid posed any real threat to a man who lived by his skill with his guns.

'You, Marshal,' the bounty hunter said. He threw his leg over the neck of his horse and slid to the ground. 'I bin hired to kill ya.'

Fallen tilted his head. 'Who hired you?'

The bounty hunter pushed the tails of his fur coat over the grips of his guns and smiled. 'That don't matter none. What does matter is that I'm gonna do it and there ain't nobody that'll stop me.'

'Now it's you that's wrong.' Valko took two steps forward. 'You'll have to kill me first, Mr Tooley.'

Tooley raised his elbows until his large hands were directly above his holstered six-shooters. 'Pleasure.'

The Kid saw the bounty hunter's hands drop and grab at the guns. He saw them clear their holsters and only then did he draw his own .45s. Bullets cut through the air in both directions as both men cocked and fired each of their weapons.

As the choking gunsmoke drifted down Front Street on the cool night air the Valko Kid stared at the dead man lying in front of him. Then he holstered his Colts.

The sight gave him no pleasure.

He turned and stared at the pair of lawmen who were looking back at him in awe. Neither had ever seen anyone draw and discharge guns so quickly before.

'Glory be!' Elmer gasped. 'Ya sure are fast with them guns and no mistake.'

Valko inhaled deeply. 'You better get that wound tended, Marshal Fallen.'

A stunned Fallen nodded silently. He could not think of anything to say. He turned and walked towards the open doorway with Elmer at his side.

The Kid glanced at the body of Black Jasper Tooley again. He gritted his teeth at the sight of steam rising from the bullet holes in the man's girth.

Silently he followed both men into the doctor's office.

FINALE

Dawn came early to War Smoke. Its blazing sun began to bake away all memories of the brutal storm of the day and night before. Yet the blood remained as the men from the funeral parlour went about their work and started to retrieve the bodies of all those who had tried and failed to defeat Matt Fallen and the two men who had stood beside him.

The Valko Kid stood next to the cot where Clem Everett lay propped up against three pillows. Everett's entire body was covered in bandages yet, even weakened, the veteran still tried to convince Fallen of his young friend's innocence. Fallen stood like a statue inside the doctor's parlour with his arm in a sling after having Colby Master's bullet cut from his shoulder. He did not speak and simply listened to every single word the retired marshal uttered.

'Now do you understand, Matt? Do you?' the

152

wounded Everett asked.

Fallen still did not say a word. He just continued to watch the young man whom he still found it impossible to comprehend. The outlaw he had read about was nothing like the Valko Kid he had seen in action. Why on earth would an outlaw risk his own life to save that of a lawman? The question taunted Fallen.

'Valko never done any of the bad things he's bin branded as doing,' Everett repeated. 'There's another varmint out there who pretends to be him. One day me and the Kid will catch that evil bastard and clear Valko's name.'

Doc Weaver leaned over his old friend. 'Don't go getting yourself all fired up, Clem. You have to take it easy for a couple of months.'

Everett looked at the old medical man and smiled. 'OK, Theo. I'll calm down.'

Doc patted his pal on the head. 'Good boy.'

Fallen opened the door, walked through the office and out into the street. He sat down on a rickety chair beside the office window and touched his injured arm. The street was busy now that the sun of a new day had returned to War Smoke. Men, women and children all nodded to the lawman, who smiled at every gesture. Yet the nagging question of who in his town had hired Black Jasper Tooley to kill him dogged his thoughts.

Which of them wanted him dead?

Then Fallen heard the tread of boots beside him as Valko walked out on to the boardwalk. The Kid said nothing as he looked down at the seated marshal. Then the undertaker's ornate hearse slowly passed before the doctor's office, led by a black horse with a matching plume on its head.

The outlaw ran a concerned finger around his own neck as he gazed at the bodies stacked inside the glass-sided hearse. The blank, expressionless faces of Tooley and Masters pressed against the glass chilled the young man. The marshal noticed the unease of the man who stood a few feet from where he was seated.

'Troubled, Mr Edwards?' Fallen asked.

Valko smiled. 'A little troubled, Marshal.'

'Why?'

'You listened to Clem long and hard in there but I never heard one word from you.' The Kid sighed as his eyes tracked the vehicle on its way back to the funeral parlour. 'I reckon that means you're gonna arrest me after all. Then I'll get myself strung up. That tends to make a man feel a little troubled.'

'We sure got a lot of good ropes in War Smoke.' Fallen pushed his hat back off his face and stared at the young man who was said to be the most blood-thirsty outlaw in the West. A statement which the marshal found hard to accept.

Valko was about to speak again when he saw Elmer

heading along Front Street towards them, leading the familiar white stallion by the reins. He rested a hand on the porch upright and smiled at the stallion.

'Snow,' Valko said.

'Mighty fine horse,' Fallen observed.

'Yep,' the Kid agreed.

Elmer reached the boardwalk and tossed the reins into the hands of the suprised Kid. The deputy sat down on the boardwalk steps and looked at his superior. 'I washed the blood off the saddle just like ya told me, Marshal Fallen,' Elmer said, grinning.

Fallen nodded. 'Well done, Elmer.'

Valko looked at the marshal. 'I don't understand. I thought you always followed the rule of law, Marshal. This don't make any sense.'

'Sure it does, Mr Edwards,' Fallen argued. 'It's what we call horse sense.'

Elmer chuckled.

The Kid could see that his rested stallion was getting excited as its powerful head bobbed up and down. He toyed with the reins in his hands and continued to look at Fallen.

'Are you gonna let me go?'

'Yep,' the marshal answered.

'But I'm a wanted outlaw.'

'No! No! No! The Valko Kid is a wanted outlaw,' Fallen corrected.

'You're Mr Edwards,' Elmer added. 'The drummer

who saved Marshal Fallen's life.'

'Twice.' Fallen grinned.

Valko swallowed hard. 'You mean I'm free to go?'

'Get going, Mr Edwards,' Fallen said firmly with a dismissive wave of his hand. 'I surely hate drummers. They're nothing but trouble. The sooner you leave my town the happier I'll be.'

'Drummers are real bothersome and no mistake.' Elmer added his dime's worth.

The Kid pulled the reins and Snow moved closer to the boardwalk where his master stood. Valko jumped across the distance between himself and his horse and landed squarely on the saddle. He poked his boots into his stirrups, gathered up his reins and turned the stallion until he was facing both men. He cleared his throat.

'Can you do me a little favour, Marshal?'

'Depends.'

'Can you tell old Clem that I'll meet up with him in two months time at Sioux City?' the Kid asked.

'We'll tell him, Mr Edwards,' Fallen declared.

'We surely will.' Elmer touched his hat.

'Thanks,' Valko said.

The two lawmen watched as Valko eased the powerful stallion away from the boardwalk and walked the animal slowly along the length of Front Street until they reached the corner where the bakery stood. For some reason Valko did not fully understand he stopped his horse and stared at the scarred wall of the building where Tooley's bullets had come close to killing him. He was about to steer his horse away and continue his journey out of town when the door of the bakery opened and again the scent of fresh bread filled Valko's nostrils.

The baker walked with a tray filled with his wares to where the horseman sat astride his mount. The man paused and looked up at the Kid.

Valko touched his hat brim. 'Howdy.'

'You going someplace, Mr Edwards?' the baker asked.

Valko nodded. 'Yep.'

'I'm sorry,' the baker said, then briefly glanced up at a small window directly above the bakery door.

The Kid held his reins firmly in his hands as his own eyes drifted to where the baker was looking. To his utter surprise he saw something he had never expected. A small boy with curly hair looked down at him from behind the grubby glass panes. Valko felt his heart quicken. He looked back at the baker.

'Tell me, friend, is his mother's name Mary?'

There was a long pause before the baker replied. 'It is.'

Valko's heart sank. He held on to his reins as the baker continued on down the street. He looked up at the child again and touched the brim of his hat. The boy waved and smiled in innocent response.

It was a smile the Kid recognized. It was Mary's smile.

The Kid fought every heart-breaking emotion inside him and turned Snow away from the bakery. The stallion reared up and kicked out with its forelegs as if in salute to the child before taking its master down the long busy street.

Inside the small room the boy kept on waving as the rider slowly guided his horse away from the building.

'There's a man down there on the most beautiful white horse I ever seen, Mommy,' the child said. 'Come look.'

'What does the man look like, Bobby?'

'Like a man,' the boy answered. 'He's got black clothes on though.'

Feebly, Mary White moved slowly across the room to her son. It required all of her once abundant strength just to reach him. Her hands were wrapped around him like a protective blanket as she pulled him close to her.

'Who is he, Mommy?'

Her fingers ran through the boy's hair. 'A friend, Bobby. A true friend.'

'What's his name?'

'The Valko Kid,' Mary whispered.

Valko felt as though he were being torn apart by invisible chains as he headed his stallion towards the edge of town. Chains which could not be seen, but they were there all the same, mercilessly ripping at his soul. Yet the Kid knew that he had to ride away. He had to keep going to ensure the boy would remain safe.

Just as he reached the last of War Smoke's buildings, Valko twirled the long ends of his reins to urge the stallion to find even greater pace. He cracked the reins at the ground. It sounded like a whip.

The white horse thundered away from War Smoke.

'Ride, Snow. Ride faster than you've ever done before,' Valko called out, his voice breaking.

As always the white horse obeyed its master. Soon only a cloud of dust from the hoofs of the magnificent stallion remained hanging on the morning air.

Then the Valko Kid was gone.